# Sammy in Ireland

## Single Wide Female Travels
## Book 5

By

Lillianna Blake

ISBN: 0692739661
ISBN-13: 978-0692739662

# DEDICATION

To all women out there who are looking
for their pot of gold. ☺

# TABLE OF CONTENTS

# CHAPTER 1

The dim glow of the airplane's floor lights had become familiar to me. With so much travel under my belt, getting to the plane on time, enduring unruly passengers, and finding a comfortable way to sleep during a flight had become second nature to me. But I didn't want to sleep.

I was excited about landing in Dublin. Of all the places I'd visited, Ireland was the most mystical to me. Its beauty had charmed me from the time I was a young girl.

Max, on the other hand, was quite content to be snoring away beside me.

I looked over at him and admired the way his lips moved in his slumber. Of all the adventures I'd experienced, my relationship with Max had been the most rewarding. After a few hiccups during our time in London, it had become my mission to ensure that our relationship wasn't getting lost in the midst of my career.

I pulled out the journal where I'd started writing an

open dialogue with myself about my marriage. It was a safe place to express what I was feeling so that I didn't always bottle it up. It was also an ideal way to figure out if the worry or frustration I sometimes felt was a result of Max's actions, or something deeper within me that needed to be worked through.

As I began to journal about my expectations for Ireland, I noticed a theme in my writing. I wanted it to be magical—from start to finish. Maybe I was putting too much pressure on the trip. We had a few extra days to spend together—just the two of us—and that was like a fantasy to me. No interruptions—just Max and Sammy time.

Even though we'd been traveling together, it was sometimes difficult to get that alone time when we could just focus on each other. With my book tour picking up steam and the popularity of my blog increasing, there was always extra work to do.

So I made a promise—to my journal and to myself— that I would make my marriage a priority and spend our few days of freedom engaged with the amazing man that I'd married.

As I tucked the journal away and closed my eyes, it hit me once more—the acknowledgement of the way that my life had taken off. From no motivation, to nothing but movement.

The plane touched down in Ireland and my imagination started to go wild with possibilities. There were so many things to explore.

I slipped my hand into Max's and leaned over to kiss his cheek. "We're here, Max. We made it."

He opened his eyes with a sleepy smile and nodded. "I'm glad." He kissed me quickly on the lips before he stood up to gather our carry-on bags.

I took the time to admire him yet again. Max had been the one constant in my life, a dream come true for me, not through skill or demand, but because I'd opened my heart and allowed our love to blossom. I hoped that I could continue to keep that open heart.

"Are you excited? I'm so excited!" For once I forgot about being subdued on a plane.

"I'm all about the green beer." Max smiled.

"Green beer?" I raised an eyebrow. "Is that the only thing you're excited about?"

"Not at all." He laughed. "But the look on your face just then was worth it."

"Stop teasing me, Max." I didn't have time to be exasperated, as the passengers on the plane all wanted off at the same time. I enjoyed hearing the mixture of accents and languages that I often heard on the plane. It was on my list of to-dos while in Ireland to learn a few Gaelic phrases.

Once we collected our luggage and were out of the airport, the reality of where we'd landed really struck me. Ireland's brooding skies and expansive greens were not exactly reflected in the busy streets of Dublin. But the architecture still enchanted me. I snapped a few pictures through the window of the taxi on our way to the hotel.

"I have a feeling I'm going to be seeing that camera instead of your beautiful face." Max laughed and patted my knee. "We'll have plenty of time for photographs."

"No way, Max, you're going to be seeing a lot more of me than that."

"Oh, really?" He grinned. "Do tell me more."

"Max, you're so silly."

"Am I?" He kissed my cheek. "I guess we'll find out."

The taxi rolled to a stop outside a small hotel surrounded by other buildings. Max stepped out and held the door for me so I could follow. He paid the driver, then gathered the bags. I grabbed a few from his hands.

"I can carry them." He frowned.

"I know you can, but you shouldn't have to carry everything."

He met my eyes and grinned. "I see where you're going with this, but it's my privilege and pleasure to carry your bags."

"Have you been reading *One Hundred and One Sweet Things to Say to Your Wife* again?"

He shrugged and winked, then led the way into the hotel.

Once we were registered we took the elevator to our floor. I rested my head against the back of the elevator for a moment and yawned.

"Are you okay, Sammy?"

"Sure. We can just put our bags down, and then we can start exploring."

"You don't want to rest a little first?"

I stifled another yawn and shook my head. "I'll be fine. I can't wait to get out there." I leaned a bit on Max's arm as we left the elevator for the room.

Once inside, I sat down on the edge of the bed and smiled. "We're here."

"Yes, we are." Max sat down beside me and wrapped his arm around my shoulders. "So what do you want to do first?"

There were a million ideas on the tip of my tongue but when I opened my mouth I yawned again. "Maybe I just need to stretch out for a minute."

"Good idea." He sprawled out on the bed beside me.

As I struggled to stay awake, Max was no help. He stroked my cheeks and brushed his fingertips through my hair. The more he soothed me, the more comfortable the bed felt. My eyes fluttered closed and, just before I fell asleep, I realized that Dublin would have to wait.

# CHAPTER 2

I woke a few hours later to a light soft touch across my cheek. It took me a moment to put together where I was, let alone what was touching my cheek. As my senses cleared, I smelled the lovely scent of a rose and gazed up into Max's warm eyes.

"Morning, beautiful."

"Thank you so much, Max." I took the flower and sat up slowly on the bed. With sleep still clinging to my thoughts it took me some time to process my surroundings. "How long was I out?"

"Don't worry about that, you needed your rest. I ordered some breakfast." He placed a tray on the bed beside me. It was covered with fluffy pancakes and assorted chopped fruit.

"This looks delicious. Were you bored out of your mind while I was sleeping?"

"No. I kept myself entertained by updating the blog and returning some e-mails. It seems you have quite a few fans in Ireland."

"I can't wait to meet them." I stretched my arms out

above my head and yawned. "I feel so much better. Thanks for letting me sleep."

"I got a few hours myself, so when you're ready to explore, I'll be ready too."

"Oh, I do have that meeting this morning with Fiona. Other than that, I'm free."

"Okay, I'll take a shower and get us unpacked while you're at the meeting. Then we can get started on our adventure."

"Perfect." I closed my eyes for a moment and savored the excitement that bubbled up within me.

"Right after we share this lovely breakfast." Max crawled into bed beside me and picked up a fork.

"So do you have any ideas of what you want to do today?" I asked.

"I know there are some great museums to check out. That's a good way to fill the day, since it's going to rain."

"Did you check the weather?"

"Yes. Chance of rain every day." He smiled. "Welcome to Ireland."

"I can't wait to see the countryside. I'm going to enjoy Dublin, but I'm looking forward to seeing some green too."

"Honestly, I can't quite believe that we're here. It's going to take some convincing. Never did I think I'd have the chance to visit Ireland, especially with you."

"I plan to make the best of it, rain or no rain. Maybe tonight we can catch a dinner theater. Then we'll figure out what to do tomorrow."

"Sounds great. Let me get this out of the way." He cleared the tray as I climbed out of bed.

"I could get used to this, Max."

"Me serving you breakfast in bed?"

"Yes." I smiled. "But also just this. The two of us relaxing and spending time together. I thought this book tour would give us plenty of time to connect, but it's been busy."

"Not any more." He set the tray down and walked over to me. "Now we have some time to just be together. It's what makes any country we're in the best place to be."

"Mm-hm—that book again." I kissed him hard on the lips, then pulled away before he could tackle me onto the bed. "I have to get ready to go. We'll have to work this out later."

"Promise?" He quirked a brow.

"Promise."

After I took a quick shower and dressed, I stepped out of the hotel. It was as gray as it had been when I'd stepped in, but the streets were busier. As I walked along, I noted many similarities and many differences with the streets back home. The architecture seemed older and unique, but much of the merchandise I saw in the windows of the shops was the same. The sidewalks were just as populated, but the people didn't seem to be in as much of a rush.

I made it to the address that my Ireland contact had e-mailed me and found myself in front of an old style pub. It surprised me that she'd want to meet there, but even through her e-mails Fiona seemed like a very surprising person.

I pushed open the door to the pub and peered inside. It was so early that there weren't too many patrons; however, there was one woman at the end of the bar.

I walked toward her with an eager smile. "Hi, Fiona?" I touched her shoulder.

The woman spun around and looked up at me with wide eyes. "No, sorry. Are you lost?"

"No, I'm sorry. I didn't mean to disturb you. I'm meeting someone, and I just thought you might be her."

The woman smiled and turned back to the bartender.

"Can I get you anything?" he asked.

"No, thank you. I think I'll wait until my friend arrives." I took a seat a few stools away and tried to relax. I had arrived a few minutes early. I just needed to be patient.

As I sat alone at the bar it reminded me of other times I'd been in the same position. In my younger days I'd tried the bar scene for dating on a handful of occasions. I'd quickly discovered that it was not my cup of tea or mug of beer. If anything, I'd ended up feeling more alone while I'd sat there waiting for someone to notice me. But those days were over, and my new leaf included a healthy amount of confidence.

To kill the time, I pulled out my journal and decided to write out my feelings about my morning with Max. As I wrote, I drew some comparisons to how I'd felt with Max in the past. I'd been awkward at times and a bit frightened, uncertain of whether I could be completely honest with him. Although he'd always been my closest friend and I'd trusted him with anything, when it had come to my feelings for him, I'd done my best to keep them hidden. Perhaps in some ways I was still in the habit of hiding.

LILLIANNA BLAKE

# CHAPTER 3

"There she is!"

A cry came from the door of the pub.

I jumped at the sudden sound and closed the journal. When I turned to see who it was, I saw a beautiful boisterous woman. She wore clothes with so much sparkle that it was hard to tell where the shirt and the pants separated. As she walked toward me, I admired her determined gait. She was a beautiful big woman, exactly whom I wrote for.

"Sammy!" She stretched her arms out wide. "Can I get a hug, bud?"

I held back a laugh. Her attitude was a little over the top, but that didn't mean I didn't like it.

I smiled and embraced her with a warm hug. "It's so good to meet you, Fiona."

"It's so funny to hear you say that, because I feel as if I already know you." She grasped my shoulders and looked into my eyes. "You have inspired me in so many ways, Samantha. I can't even begin to thank you."

"That's so nice of you. I'm glad that I've been able to

help in some way. That's what I hope for."

She gestured to the bar. "Please sit. Did Nick take care of you?"

"I thought I'd wait until you arrived."

"Don't get the wrong idea. I know it probably seems early to you to meet in a pub, but around here pubs are the coffee houses. Anything you like, Nick can get it for you."

"She's right." Nick tossed a towel over his shoulder and smiled at us. "So, Fiona—your usual?"

"Yes, please."

"And for you, super star?" He met my eyes.

I couldn't help but smile wider. "I'll just have an ice water."

"Just an ice water?"

"Put some lemon in it, Nick. Liven it up for Samantha." Fiona winked at him.

"That would be lovely." I nodded and tried to swallow back the nervous energy that tickled at the back of my throat. Just once I wanted to make it through a meeting without anything disastrous happening.

"I guess we should get down to business." She settled on the stool next to mine. "I have two book signings scheduled here in Dublin. Now, as I understand it, you're going to travel a bit. So if you feel the urge to host some impromptu meetings, please feel free. All I care about is your message getting out."

"I appreciate that, I really do. But I don't think I will

be doing anything extra. I'm really looking forward to spending some time with my husband—just the two of us."

"I bet. I've seen that handsome hubby of yours on your website, and he's well worth the investment."

"Thank you." I laughed. "I'll let him know that you think so."

"You'd better not!" She squealed with laughter. "I knew you were going to be so much fun to be around. Thanks, Nick." She pulled a towering glass toward her.

I couldn't quite figure out what was in the glass. It had the color of honey but didn't look like beer. It also had an assortment of olives and grapes scattered throughout the drink.

"Do you want to try some?" She smiled at me. "It's my own special concoction."

"Oh no, it's a little too early for me." I smiled and nodded at Nick as I took my glass of water. There was a small wedge of lemon on the edge of the glass.

"No, no. It doesn't have any alcohol in it. I call it my wake-me-up juice. I have a little trouble getting going in the morning, but I'm on this anti-coffee kick. It's a mixture of teas and a little bit of fruit juice. I throw the olives in there because they're my favorite and it seems to disturb people." She covered her mouth as she laughed. "I've got a devilish side."

"It sounds to me like you just enjoy having a good time." I picked up my glass of water and took a sip. As soon as the water hit my tongue my lips puckered and my eyes burned. The tiny wedge of lemon on the side of the glass was not the only lemon in the water. It also seemed to have a bit of something else mixed in. I tried not to cough but I couldn't help it.

"Are you alright there, Sammy? Maybe a little too much kick?" She patted my back. "If you can't handle the water, I'm not sure you should sample the liquor."

"Mm, too much lemon." I struggled to get my cough under control.

"Sorry, that's my fault. Nick is used to making my creative drinks. When I say lemon water, it usually means a detox version with pure lemon and a spot of honey."

"Detox?" I grabbed a napkin and wiped my mouth.

"Yes. I've tried a few fads. As much as I love my body, I have hopes of slimming down one day. I'm not sure the detox drink was very effective for me, though." She laughed.

"They can be quite dangerous to your health too."

"I see you are proving that." Fiona grinned. "Nick, I meant regular lemon water."

"Sure you did." Nick pointed at her. "You never mean regular anything, Fiona."

"That's true. It's my belief that anything can be better with a bit of a kick.

"Anyway, I don't want to hold you up. I've e-mailed you the dates and places, and of course all of my numbers in case you need to reach me."

"Thank you. I'll be sure to confirm with you."

"What are you and your husband going to do with your time in Dublin?"

"I think we're going to check out a dinner theater tonight."

"Oh?" She shrugged. "That sounds nice. I can tell you though, there's a great place that you should go. I'll text you the address."

"What is it?" I smiled.

"Let it be a surprise—trust me. It's a local place that no tourists know about."

"Should I be going then? I wouldn't want to offend anyone."

"You're not a tourist, you're an official guest. If I invited you, then you belong there." She clapped my shoulder with a thick hand. "You'll both have a great time—unless hurling is more your speed? I can get you in on some great private groups."

"Hurling?" I blinked as images of drinking far too much filled my mind.

"You know—the sport." She pulled her hand back by her shoulder then thrust it hard up through the air.

"Oh!" I laughed and shook my head. "No, I'm not sure I'm fit enough for that yet."

"It takes a certain kind of strength." Fiona nodded. "It's not for everyone. My mother said I was born to be a hurler. Not professionally of course, but I do enjoy it now and then."

"I'd love to see you do it sometime."

"Really?" She grinned. "I can make that happen. But for now, enjoy your time in Dublin."

She picked up the concoction she'd ordered and chugged down the entire glass—olives, grapes, and all.

# CHAPTER 4

Not to be outdone, I picked up my glass of lemon water with the intention of chugging it. As soon as the water hit my tongue I choked again—this time more than the last. I grabbed a napkin but before I could get it to my mouth some of the lemon water sprayed out. Fiona ducked out of the way just in time, as the water sprayed across the bar stool and landed on the wall.

"Oh no, I'm so sorry, let me get that. I didn't get you, Fiona, did I?" I jumped up with the napkin to wipe up the wall as I was treated to Fiona and Nick's laughter.

"Yes, you're going to need to toughen up a bit." Fiona gave me a playful punch to the shoulder.

"Don't worry about that, I'll get it," Nick said. "It's not the first time and it won't be the last." He pointed to a small poster of a target. "Why do you think that's there?"

I tried to laugh with them, but I was embarrassed. My first day in Dublin was not off to the best start. But instead of letting myself spiral down into the idea that the entire trip was going to be rough, I took a deep breath and accepted a glass of what I hoped was plain water from Nick. I took a long swallow and was relieved to find no lemon taste on my tongue.

"Sorry again, guys."

"Don't be. I admire a competitive spirit. Welcome to Ireland, Sammy." Fiona gave me a quick hug.

I laughed as I pulled away. Despite my mistake, Fiona still made me feel at home.

As I headed back to the hotel, my mind churned with thoughts about what was to come. Maybe I could talk Max into some Irish dancing.

I was halfway to the hotel when I noticed a slight shift in the air around me. I glanced up at the heavy sky just in time to get smacked in the face by a big fat raindrop. I groaned as I realized that I'd forgotten to bring an umbrella. Even though Max had warned me that it was going to rain, I hadn't taken the time to bring the one thing that would keep me dry.

That one raindrop was followed by a downpour. It only took a few moments for my clothes to become soaked. All around me the sidewalks emptied.

A young man ran across the street toward me with an umbrella in hand.

"Here, miss, can I walk you somewhere?"

"No, it's okay. I'll just pick one up in this shop. Thank you, though." I smiled at him. Already I had the impression that Ireland could be a very friendly place.

I pulled the door to the shop open and stepped inside. An old man sat on a stool behind a small counter. He smiled and revealed teeth in dire need of dental care.

"Caught in the wet, are you?"

"Yes, I'm afraid so. Do you have any umbrellas?"

"Ah yes, big business around here. There's some in the corner over there."

I walked over to the assortment of umbrellas and selected what I hoped would be the largest. As I lugged it over to the counter I still kicked myself for being so foolish. I set the umbrella on the counter and dug through my bag to find my wallet. I had so many things inside that it was hard to get to.

"American, are you?" He smiled.

"Yes." I offered a small smile. "Can you tell?"

"The accent gives it away."

I grinned at the thought that I had an accent when his lilt was so melodic to my ears. "Just a moment, it's in here somewhere."

"No charge. Just take it. No one around here is going to buy that one anyway."

"Oh? Why not?"

"Just watch out for the wind. It gives a lot of coverage, but if the wind blows, you might float away like Mary Poppins."

"Thanks for the advice and the umbrella." I handed him a business card that I managed to fish out. "Let me know if there's a way I can repay your kindness."

He chuckled and shook his head. "No, no, sweet lass. Kindness is free." He took the card and nodded his head toward the door. "Better get on your way before you need a boat."

"Thanks again." I waved to him and left the shop with a smile.

The thought of my floating anywhere kept me amused as I struggled to get the umbrella open. I held tight to it and continued down the sidewalk toward the hotel.

# CHAPTER 5

What I expected to be an easy walk, turned out to be a rather harsh one. As the shop owner had predicted, the winds had picked up quite a bit. I tried to keep my grip on the umbrella but the wooden handle slipped through my wet hands. It was hard to see what was in front of me, and I began to wonder if I'd already walked past the hotel without realizing it. Was I going to end up lost in Dublin on my first day?

I let go of the umbrella with one hand in an attempt to get my phone out of my purse. At that moment, a burst of wind blew under the umbrella and ripped it right up out of my hands. I lunged to grab it, but it skidded down a flooded alley. I could have gone after it, but I didn't want to soak my feet in whatever swirled around in the water. Now, even the kindness that I'd been given had been taken away. I had no idea what I'd done so wrong to get myself into such a predicament, until I remembered—I'd forgotten to bring an umbrella.

I ducked my head into the rain and continued

forward. A few minutes later I spotted an umbrella ahead of me. It was held by someone standing in front of the hotel. As I walked toward the hotel the rain let up enough that I could see clearly through it.

"Max!"

"There you are! I've been calling." He walked up to me and did his best to shield me with the umbrella.

"Oh, thanks, but there's not much point now. I'm sopping wet. I'm sorry. My phone must be in the bottom of my bag and I didn't hear it ring. I can't believe I forgot an umbrella, even after you warned me it would rain."

He smiled so wide that I caught a glimmer of his teeth.

"Max, there's no need to rub it in. I know I was foolish."

He shook his head. "That's not why I'm smiling."

"Then why?" I stared at him with wide eyes. "What about this situation could make you smile?"

"You look so beautiful." He trailed a fingertip through a tendril of my rain-soaked hair. "I can't help it."

I couldn't help but smile in return. "Thank you. The rain isn't so bad, really. It's kind of nice."

He folded up his umbrella and gazed into my eyes. "Then maybe we should both enjoy it."

"Max! You'll be soaked!"

He held my eyes. "I don't care." His arms slid around me and the rain pelted down on us.

When he kissed me, with streams of water trailing

along both our faces, I experienced a sensation that I hadn't had in a long time. I felt young and playful again. I felt in love and excited again.

He held me close as he deepened the kiss.

I thought about how annoyed I'd been for not remembering my umbrella—and then how remarkable it was to suddenly be enjoying such a spectacular moment with Max.

When he finally broke the kiss he rested his forehead against mine. "This isn't the first time we've kissed the rain."

"And it won't be the last." I kissed him again. "I guess we'll need a shower and a change before we start exploring."

"We might need a bit more than that." He kissed me again.

By the time we actually left our hotel room again, it was mid-afternoon. I didn't mind at all. Our time together had been amazing. As I walked hand in hand with Max toward the museums, the sidewalk could have been made from clouds. Despite a rough start to the morning, I was in full fantasyland and couldn't have been happier.

We breezed through a few of the museums and shared a late lunch.

"You never did tell me about your meeting with Fiona."

"Let's just say it was invigorating." I laughed. "I think

she's a very interesting woman. She's definitely enthusiastic."

"Well, that's a good thing, right?"

"I think so. She told me about a great place to go tonight."

"What is it?" He met my eyes across the table.

"I'm not really sure. She didn't tell me much about it. She just said it was a place I had to go."

"And you trust her?"

"I'm sure she wouldn't steer me in the wrong direction. And not you, either. She's quite fond of you."

"Me?" He laughed. "I don't even know her."

"You don't know her, but she knows you. She's a fan of both of us."

"Well, that's nice to hear. I guess we should check this place out. No dinner theater, then?"

"No, I think this will be more fun. Locals always know the best places to visit."

"Good point." He grinned. "Alright, do you want to hit some of the shops when we're done here?"

"Great idea! I want to go back to one in particular and thank a man for an umbrella."

"But you didn't have an umbrella." He quirked a brow. "You were soaked."

"That's because my umbrella blew away. But I still want to thank him. He said something to me that really made an impression...Kindness is free."

"That's a sweet sentiment." Max finished the last bite

of his sandwich. "I wish more people believed that."

"Have you experienced something different?" I scooped up the last forkful of my salad.

"In my experience—present company excluded, of course—people rarely give freely. They expect something in return—something more than a thank you. Don't get me wrong, people are still helpful, but there seems to be an exchange required."

"I don't think there's anything wrong with that. I mean, it keeps the balance, right? Giving and receiving? Otherwise people can start to feel taken advantage of, don't you think?"

"I think that may be true in some ways. But it's not quite kindness if you expect something in return, is it? I think to be kind, you have to do something from your heart, without expectation of anything in return. But I haven't exactly fulfilled that myself. Not very often, anyway."

"You do for me all the time." I smiled. "Like making me breakfast and waiting for me with the umbrella. You didn't have to do any of those things."

"No, I didn't, but I'm still receiving something in return—a beautiful woman who knows how loved and appreciated she is. That's a lot to me."

"I do know that, Max." I blushed as I pushed my dish away. "Are you ready?"

"Yes, let's get to shopping. We've worked hard all this time; I'm ready to splurge. Are you?"

"Maybe just a little bit." I grinned.

## CHAPTER 6

Max and I spent the afternoon visiting many shops, but one thing I noticed about them was that they were all pretty pricey. That was to be expected, since we were in Dublin and many of the shops we were going into seemed to be tourist traps.

When we'd made it back to the shop where I'd been given the umbrella, I opened the door eager to greet the owner. Instead, there was a young woman behind the counter. While Max browsed, I decided to find out what I could about the man that had been so kind to me.

I walked up to the counter. The woman barely looked up at me.

"Hi. I was in here earlier this morning and there was a very nice gentleman working. The owner?"

"I don't think so. I'm the owner. I had an employee here this morning."

"Oh." I tried to cover my surprise. She seemed quite young to own her own business. It reminded me that women of all ages could accomplish their dreams. "I have to say he's a wonderful  employee. He treated me with such kindness."

The woman sighed and tipped her stool back some as she looked across the counter at me. "Let me guess, you're the one he gave a free umbrella to?"

"Well, yes. I came back to pay for it, though."

"Wonderful. Perhaps you can pay for all the damage that it caused as well?"

"Damage?" I raised an eyebrow. "It blew away in the storm."

"I know it blew away. It blew into someone's window, and then it blew into someone who was for some unknown reason riding a bicycle in that terrible weather, and it even blew into a newspaper stand. So, that free umbrella—since it had our store's name on it—cost us quite a bit. That's why he's not here this afternoon. He knows better than to sell those big umbrellas. They are notorious for wreaking havoc in bad weather."

"It wasn't his fault." I shook my head. "I picked it out. He warned me to be careful. It was completely my fault. I can write a check for the damage."

The woman eyed me for a moment. "Really?"

"Sure."

"Don't worry about it. The insurance will cover it. But that was quite kind of you to offer. Most people have that 'not my problem' mentality."

"Not me. He did something kind for me, and I'd hate for him to suffer any consequences because of my mistake."

"Alright, I'll take it easy on the old man."

Max walked up to the register with an assortment of items to purchase. "I've got a few things for people back home. Did you find anything?"

"I haven't really looked yet."

"Okay, we have plenty of time. Go ahead and look around."

"No, that's okay. I think I'm done shopping for today. I'm really curious about the address that Fiona gave me."

"Alright, let's head out." He handed the woman some money for the items and she bagged them up.

"Do you still need an umbrella?" She glanced at me.

"No thank you. My husband and I have one to share."

"Okay, have a nice visit."

"Thanks." I smiled at her and slipped my arm through Max's as we walked out the door. As disappointed as I was that my umbrella had caused a disaster, I was relieved that I'd stopped back in to the shop. Maybe the man who gave the umbrella to me wouldn't be in as much trouble.

The sun seemed to be setting rather fast, perhaps because of the cloudy sky. Streetlights struggled to illuminate the dimly lit streets.

"Do we need a taxi?" Max started to raise his hand to hail one.

"No, it's not far—just a few blocks this way." I gave his hand a tug. "Let's hurry before we get caught in more rain."

He laughed and quickened his pace. "I don't mind the rain."

"I bet you don't. But I don't want to wear wet clothes all night."

"No one says you have to." He grinned.

"I'm not sure nudism is customary in Ireland."

"Hm, maybe not."

After we walked for about fifteen minutes Max paused and tried to peer at my phone. "Where exactly are we going?"

"Don't worry about that, Max. I know just how to get there." I continued forward with a confident smile.

"Sammy, we're in the middle of a city we don't know, in the middle of a country we've never been to before. I'm not sure if I want to trust your sense of direction."

"Really?" I stopped and turned to look at him. "You're doubting me?"

He laughed and wrapped his arm around my waist. "Not you, darling—your sense of direction. Need I remind you of the places it's led us?"

"No, please don't." I laughed. "It is quite a long list. But just this once it would be nice if you could have a little faith in me."

He tightened his grip around me and stared into my eyes. "I will never ever lose faith in you, Sammy." He sighed and kissed my forehead. "Let's go."

LILLIANNA BLAKE

# CHAPTER 7

Warmed by Max's words, I led him toward the address on my phone. The closer we got to it, however, the less faith I had in myself—or perhaps, more accurately, in Fiona. When we ended up in a dim fragrant alley, I tightened my hand around his.

"Okay, maybe you should doubt me more often."

"This is the place?" He glanced around and then back at me. "Are you sure?"

"It's the address she sent me. Maybe I put something into the map wrong." I stared at my phone. "I didn't even type it in, though."

"I'm sure it's nothing you did. You did meet this woman at a pub first thing in the morning, right? Maybe she was a little too intoxicated to give you the right address."

"No way. She wasn't drinking at all. I'm sorry, Max." I frowned. "I guess I'm blowing our first night out in Dublin."

"None of that." He cupped my chin and drew my lips to his. After a soft slow kiss he looked into my eyes. "It

41

can't be ruined as long as we are together. It's still early. We can try to catch a movie or something. Let's go."

I was relieved that Max wasn't mad, but still disappointed that I had bungled things. As usual, I had set my expectations for our time in Ireland very high and found myself crushed at the lack of success. As we started to turn back around in the alley, a door swung open. A man stumbled out with a laugh that was followed by enchanting music.

"Max, wait!" I grabbed his arm and pulled him back. "Did you hear that?"

"Yes, I did." He stared at the door as it closed again. "I thought that was just an emergency exit. There's no sign or anything."

"She did say it's a local place that no tourists know about. Maybe that's why they don't advertise."

"Well, it sure looks like he had a good time." Max laughed as the man hung onto the wall as he made his way down the alley.

"Yes, it does. Let's check it out. It'll be fun."

"Alright, but if it's rough, we're out of there, okay?"

"For sure." I nodded.

Max held the door open for me as I stepped inside. The first thing I noticed was the smell. It was a bit stale, like spilled beer and ancient peanuts. The space was also very small, with only a few tables and a short bar. None of that mattered once I heard the music. I tightened my hand on Max's and glanced over my shoulder to smile at him.

"This is absolutely perfect."

"It's pretty great."

"Let's find a table." I led him through the few occupied tables to an empty one. There was a small stage beside the bar. An older man stood on it and sang as he played a guitar. "His voice is amazing."

"Yes, it is."

"I'm glad we found this place."

"Me too." Max smiled and opened his mouth to say more, but just then a waitress made her way over.

"What can I get for you?"

"Is there a menu?" Max glanced around at the other tables. The woman laughed and shook her head.

"No, sorry, sonny, no menus here. If you don't know what we have to offer then you must be new. You have three choices."

As she rattled off the options, I was drawn back into the music that surrounded us. It haunted me inside, as if it was a melody I held dear—even though I'd never heard it before.

"And you, miss?"

"I'll have whatever he's having." I smiled at her.

When she walked away, Max stared into my eyes. "You do realize that I ordered duck."

"Duck?" I scrunched up my nose. "No way. I'm not eating that."

"I'm kidding. I just can't get enough of the way you

crinkle your nose like that."

"Oh, really?" I shook my head. "I'm sure it'll get old eventually."

"Your nose? Maybe, but it will still be cute."

"No I meant it will get old that I crinkle it. I mean, we're still in the honeymoon phase, right?"

"Honeymoon phase?" He cleared his throat and settled his gaze on me in a way that I knew meant he wasn't pleased. "I don't think we're in any phase. We love each other, that's that."

"Right, but as time goes by, I'm sure we won't find everything that one other does so endearing."

"I will." He smiled at the waitress as she brought us both a beer.

When she walked away I leaned closer to him. "Max, you don't have to say that. I believe our relationship should be more realistic."

"Realistic?" He sighed and ran his fingertips through his hair. "What's so unrealistic about being with the most amazing woman I've ever met?"

"I just don't want you to think that you always have to compliment me."

"Sammy, I know I don't always have to compliment you. I compliment you because I look at you and a million compliments fill my mind. If I don't say at least one, my brain might just explode. Is that what you want, Samantha?" He arched a brow. "Do you not care if my brain explodes?"

"Max, stop." I laughed and grabbed his hand across the table. "You're so wonderful."

"I hope you're going to think that for the next eighty years."

"Eighty?"

"Sixty?"

"Ninety?"

"Two hundred?"

"Okay, okay, for as long as we get." I lifted my beer to toast. "To everything that is to come."

"I can definitely drink to that."

We clinked glasses and sipped our beer.

"Wow, this is delicious."

"Yes, I would say it's better than any beer I've ever had." Max took another long swallow.

The night continued on with the singer on stage serenading us and with delectable local food filling our bellies. But the part I treasured the most was my time with Max. I'd constructed so many thoughts about the future of our marriage in my head. I expected that our desire for each other would wane—that what he thought was adorable about me would eventually become what he hated.

But maybe Max was right. Maybe our relationship didn't have to follow that particular path. I decided to settle into the warmth that we shared and ignore the anticipation of the future.

# CHAPTER 8

When it was time for the bar to close, Max and I walked arm in arm back to the hotel. Luckily not a drop of rain fell, but the entire city had a hush to it. It wasn't quiet, as plenty of tourists were leaving the bars and clubs. But the way the sky enveloped everything with its heavy presence seemed to give it a sense of quiet despite the chaos.

"That was quite a night." Max held the elevator doors open for me. "I'm pretty wiped out. I just have to do a few things on the computer."

"Aw, really? You still have to work?"

"A blog never sleeps." He smiled at me. "Plus I need to make sure the website is in working order. With the book signings coming up the traffic always increases."

"Alright, I suppose I can share you with a computer screen for a little while."

"Not too long, I promise." He gave me a quick kiss before we stepped off the elevator.

I spent some time in the bathroom washing my face and changing into pajamas. While Max occupied himself at the computer, I decided to write a bit more in our relationship journal. I reached into my bag to find it. My heart dropped as the more I searched, the more certain I became that it wasn't there. For a brief moment my entire body flashed hot. Had I lost it? Could I possibly have left behind a journal that important, filled with incredibly private information about my relationship with Max? What if someone found it? What if they read it?

As the panic spread through my body I began to look in other bags. I tried to appear as casual as I could. If Max knew I'd lost something, he'd want to know what it was. I couldn't risk telling him or he might be furious. Even though Max was normally very understanding, could anyone really be understanding about their personal information being available for prying eyes to see?

"Wow, Sammy, there's been a big increase of followers on your blog. I wonder what's drawing them in?"

My throat grew dry. Could that be a coincidence? The fact that I'd lost the journal and my blog followers increased led me to the overwhelming conclusion that someone had found the journal and posted it online somewhere.

"Max, can I use the computer?"

"Sure, I've done my updates." He stood up and stopped suddenly when he looked into my eyes. "Everything alright?"

"Yes, it's fine. I just forgot about something that I

need to do."

"Okay." He narrowed his eyes. "Are you sure that you're okay?"

"Yes, Max, I'm fine."

I sat down in the chair in front of the computer and opened a search page. I began searching my name, Max's name, and every combination of our names together. There was a good amount of information in the search results, but nothing that was as personal as what I'd written in the journal. I grabbed my phone and walked toward the balcony.

"Max, I'm going to get some air."

"Want company?" He looked up from his tablet.

"No, that's okay. I'll be back in a minute."

As soon as I was alone on the balcony, I dialed Fiona's number. I held my breath as I realized how late it was. I couldn't wait until morning.

"Samantha? Is everything okay?"

"Yes, I'm so sorry to call you so late, but I think I left something important at the bar where we met today. Did the owner mention it? It was a journal."

"No, he didn't say anything and I didn't see anything. I'm sure you can call him in the morning to double check."

"Okay, yes." I sighed and closed my eyes.

"Samantha, what was in the journal?"

"My life, Max's life, way too much personal information. I have to get it back."

"I'll call Nick first thing in the morning and ask him about it. Are you sure you left it there?"

"I think it's the only place I could have." My blood ran cold as I recalled digging through my purse at the small shop. Was it possible that I took it out and left it on the counter? I cringed at the thought. That would mean that anyone could have it.

"I'm not sure, to be honest."

"Try not to worry too much. It'll turn up."

I hung up the phone with a heavy feeling in my heart. Would it turn up? If it did, would it turn up in the wrong hands?

# CHAPTER 9

As much as I tried, I couldn't sleep. Every time I started to fall into slumber, I would remember the lost journal and wake up with a rush of heat in my cheeks. How would I ever explain this to Max?

I gave up on staying in bed and settled myself in front of the computer again. Through bleary eyes I tried to scour the Internet. If someone had posted something online about me, I was sure one of my fans would have come across it by now.

I didn't find anything about my journal entries. What I did find were horror stories about people's personal information being exposed.

I forced myself to leave the computer just as the sun rose. I grabbed my phone and stepped out onto the balcony again. As soon as I dialed Fiona's number, she picked up.

"Sorry to bother you again. Did you have a chance to call Nick?"

"Yes, I did. I'm sorry, but he said that he didn't find

any notebooks. Are you sure you left it there?"

"No, I'm not." I sighed and closed my eyes. "I guess I'm out of luck. Soon all of Dublin will know about my worries over Max and my desire to be more affectionate with him."

"Oh, is that all? I thought there might be some explicit things in there."

"Well, no, not exactly explicit."

"Just take a breath, Samantha. Did you put your name in the journal?"

"No. No, I didn't."

"Okay, then if someone finds it, they won't even know who it belongs to."

"You don't think so?"

"No, I don't. Now don't let this ruin your fun. There's so much you and Max can enjoy today. Try to forget about it, okay? If it turns up at the pub, I'll call you right away."

"You're right. I guess I overreacted. Thanks, Fiona."

I hung up the phone and looked out at the sunrise. It wasn't much of one, watered down by the thick clouds, but it was still beautiful. I reminded myself that I was in Dublin, and I needed to embrace my moment instead of focusing on a mistake. Maybe Max would find out, maybe he wouldn't, but until then I could have a great time and so could he.

When I stepped back into the hotel room, Max stirred and looked over at me.

"Are you up early?"

"Not exactly." I offered a short laugh.

"You never slept?" He sat up in the bed. "Are you sick?"

"No, I'm not sick. I just couldn't seem to sleep. I guess I'm too excited to be here."

"We can stay in bed for a while if you want. You need your rest."

"No way, I'm ready to hit the town with you."

"Hm." He stretched and yawned. "I guess the snuggling will have to wait." He climbed out of bed and made his way to the bathroom.

I dressed while I waited for him. With every piece of clothing I put on, I recognized that I was also feeling that way emotionally. I wanted to protect my thoughts and concerns from the eyes of others, just like I wanted to shield my body from the views of others. Something Fiona said struck a chord with me. Why was I so worried about what I'd written? My thoughts likely weren't much different than any other woman's in a relationship. Maybe this was a hint that I needed to be a little more free and open with my emotions.

Once we were off to explore Dublin for the day, it was pretty easy for me to forget about the missing journal. We toured some historical buildings that transported me back through time. I wondered what it might have been like for a woman to live during a time when women had very little freedom. I wouldn't have had the option to marry or not in some cases, and certainly wouldn't have been able to have a career.

"Look at this, Max." I pointed out a Claddagh ring on display. "Isn't it beautiful?"

"Yes, it is. I've always liked those." He snapped a picture of it with his phone.

"Now who is the picture hound?" I grinned.

"I just want to remember it. Sometimes I forget about things so easily." He paused and looked into my eyes. "I just want to make sure we don't forget these experiences."

"How could we?"

We left the building and started down the street toward a pub.

"Time goes by so fast, you know? It's easy to believe that we'll remember every little detail, but there are things that seemed so important to me at one time and now I barely remember why." Max said.

"That's true. I remember when the highlight of my day was folding laundry."

"I remember that too." He grinned. "I used to like to spend my time there with you."

"Do you still like that, Max?"

"Of course I do."

"I just feel like we're always doing stuff I like. Isn't there anything that you'd like to do?"

"I like historical things. I like museums."

"Don't be difficult, Max, you know what I mean."

"Difficult?" He gasped. "Me?"

I raised an eyebrow. "I just want to be sure you're happy."

"I am, sweetheart." He turned to face me. "I am. I just wish you wouldn't worry so much."

I bit into my bottom lip. There it was again—my insecurity rearing its ugly head. I really needed to find a way to get that under control.

I took a deep breath, determined to throw myself into the day.

# CHAPTER 10

When we stepped into the pub I noticed that there was quite a crowd. We picked a spot as out of the way as possible, then sat down to eat.

When the waitress brought our menus, she wore a huge smile.

"Hi, I'm so glad to be your waitress today. What can I get you to eat?"

"I'd love whatever the special is." I smiled in return. "I want to try something new today."

"Oh, great idea. Trying something new is a great way to spice up your life—and your relationship." She winked at me.

My cheeks grew hot. One of the things I'd recently written about in my journal was my desire to try new things with Max. Was it possible that somehow this waitress knew this?

"Absolutely." Max nodded. "Can't let things get boring—not when there's so much to explore. I'll have what she's having, please."

The waitress nodded and walked away.

I looked across the table at Max.

"That was a little odd, wasn't it?"

"What?" He looked away from the window and back to me.

"Just that she would say something like that to us."

"I don't think so. People seem more friendly and open here. Maybe she was just trying to make conversation."

"Maybe."

"Did it bother you?" He reached across the table and took my hand.

"No, not really."

"You're blushing." He grinned.

"It's not what you think."

"No? Are things not…inventive enough for you?"

"Don't be ridiculous. You know there are no problems in that department. I mean, unless you think so."

"Not at all." He gave my hand a light squeeze. "But you're still blushing."

"That's because you're asking me these things—with other people around."

"They're not concerned about our conversation. I didn't mean to make you uncomfortable, though."

"I'm not. I'm just a little surprised. We don't usually talk about things like that."

"Maybe we should. I have a lot to say—trust me."

"Really?"

"Sure. All good things. It just seems like you might be a little uneasy discussing details. I'd love to talk about what you might want to explore, but only if you want to."

"I do. But not here." I smiled. "Is that alright?"

"Sure."

We shared a quick meal without much interruption from the waitress. But when she walked back over to clear the dishes she paused right beside me.

"Oh, I'm so glad to see that you've enjoyed the food. I think it's great when a couple can share similar tastes. Sometimes opposites just cause chaos in a relationship, don't you think?" She looked into my eyes.

"I suppose." I stammered over my reply, shocked by the question. "I think it depends on the couple. Some people make opposites work. But it is nice to have a lot in common."

"Do you ever worry that you might not have as much in common as you think? Like maybe the other person is just trying to appease you?" She tilted her head to the side.

It was as if she'd read an entire page of my journal. I was tempted to call her on it and demand that she return it. But Max's eyes were on me, and I didn't want him to know about the journal in the first place.

"I think everyone worries about that." I nodded at her.

She walked away with the dishes.

I looked across the table at Max. "That's being

friendly?"

"Sammy, I think you're reading too much into it. She's just trying to be nice."

"Nice is one thing, but commenting on things like that just feels intrusive."

"We're in a different country—a different culture."

"You're right." I laughed and shook my head. "I'm sorry. I'm being silly. I guess I'm just a little wound up today."

"What's going on with you?" He sat back in his chair. "Does something have you nervous?"

I stared at him for a long moment. Could he really be that in tune with me that he knew I was nervous about losing the journal, or was I just being quite obvious?

Luckily, before I could answer, the waitress returned with our check.

"It was great to serve you two. You know, I don't say this to many people, but you are just a great couple. I hope that one day I'll be able to find someone to love, the way that you two love one another."

My heart melted at her words. The entire meal I'd been judging, while she'd been admiring.

"I'm so sure that you will. You'll know it when it's right."

"Thanks so much. That means a lot coming from you." She cringed and looked toward the bar, then back to me. "I could really get into a lot of trouble for this, but I just can't resist. Do you think you could sign my book for me?"

My eyes widened. "I'm sorry? I'm not sure I understand."

"I know who you are." She grinned. "It's okay if you don't want to sign it. I probably shouldn't have asked."

"Of course I'll sign your book for you. It's always an honor to meet one of my readers."

"I can't wait for the next book. There will be another one, right?"

"Oh yes, I hope so." I laughed. She pulled a paperback copy of *Becoming Zara* out of her apron.

"Thanks so much for this. When I heard that you were going to be in Dublin I brought it to work with me—just in case you stopped in. Does that make me an obsessed fan?"

"Not at all. It just means you're dedicated and going for what you want. Are you coming to the book signing?"

"I wasn't able to get a ticket." She frowned.

"Here." I pulled out my business card and jotted down a note on the back of it. "Just hand this to whoever is at the door and you'll be able to get in. If you have any trouble just call the number on the card. Okay?"

"Really? Wow! Thanks so much. I can't wait."

I smiled as I signed her book, then handed it back to her. "I look forward to seeing you again. Thanks for the great service."

I breathed a sigh of relief as I realized that the reason she knew about some of my personal business was because she likely followed my blog and had definitely read the book. It was pretty easy to make assumptions, and I mentally kicked myself for being so quick to judge.

Max escorted me out the door with a playful smile on his lips. "So I guess she was nice after all?"

"Very." I rolled my eyes and shook my head. "I'm a little off kilter, that's for sure."

"Off kilter? I haven't heard that expression in a while."

"I must have kilts on my mind."

"Oh, really?" He grabbed my hand and pulled me down the street toward another shop. "Then maybe we should go in here?"

"What is this place?"

He whisked me inside before I could get a look at the sign.

# CHAPTER 11

Inside the shop it was quite dark and smoky.

"Is this place on fire or something? Why are we here?" As soon as the words left my mouth music started pounding. I jumped at the sound and grabbed Max's hand. "Max?"

"Shh. I think you're going to like it."

He led me through the smoke and I discovered three muscular men in kilts. Max handed a man behind a podium some money.

"Max, please tell me what's going on."

"Just wait." He grinned.

The men in front of me began to dance. As they danced, they began to loosen their kilts.

"Max no!" I turned my face to his chest. "I can't watch this—not with you here."

"No?" He frowned. "I thought you wanted to have more fun?"

"Not like this! Not unless it's you in the kilt."

"I thought you'd never ask." He laughed as he joined

the men in front of me.

The man behind the podium flung a kilt at him and Max wrapped it around his waist. He began to dance in time with the other three men. I couldn't help but laugh, even as I tried to ignore the heat in my cheeks and the sultry way Max flexed his hips. As the music ended and the other three men retreated, Max started to unfasten the kilt.

"Oh, no way. That's coming with us. How much?" I flashed my wallet at the man behind the podium.

"I'm not wearing it on the street, though!" Max pulled it off and folded it up.

I paid for the kilt and we made our way back through the smoke.

"So? Was that fun and inventive?" He grinned, clearly pleased with himself.

"It was very fun—and unexpected."

"I'm glad you enjoyed it."

I wrapped my arm around his and looked up into his eyes. "You never fail to surprise me, Max."

"The feeling is mutual, my love." He kissed my forehead. "I just want you to have a great time."

As we headed back toward the hotel I noticed a street vendor with some nice trinkets for sale.

"Let's stop here. I want to pick up a few more things."

I sorted through what was available and soon found a nice necklace, an assortment of magnets, and some items with Ireland's flag.

As I paid the vendor, he tipped his hat at me.

"Thanks, lass, I'm sure there's other things you could spend your money on."

"All of this is worth it."

"Remember that. Things don't have to be perfect to be priceless." He winked at me.

The words reminded me of something I'd written in my journal about feeling the need to be perfect for Max. Had the man read my words?

"What do you mean by that, sir?"

"Oh, nothing much, I just try to hand out pearls of wisdom to all of my customers. That's a good one, aye?"

"Sure is." I smiled. "Thank you." I shook my head as I realized I was still being quite paranoid. Maybe a little down time at the hotel would help me to clear my mind.

When we arrived at the hotel there was a crowd in the lobby.

"I'm going to check on our arrangements for our travel tomorrow. I'll be right up, okay?" Max kissed my cheek and handed me the bags.

"You really want to wait through all this? We can always confirm in the morning."

"In the morning it might be too late to make changes. I don't want anything to go wrong. It'll just take a few minutes, I'm sure."

"Okay." I hugged him, then walked over to the elevator.

Max was always taking care of things and I appreciated that, as my tendency toward procrastination had led to some frustrating experiences. On the way up to the hotel room I thought about the journal again. If it was gone, it was gone. Maybe I was never meant to write in it. I could have been talking to Max instead of spending all my time hiding my thoughts and emotions between pieces of paper.

I stepped off the elevator and walked down the hall to the hotel room. When I stopped in front of the door I found an envelope taped there. It was addressed to me so I pulled it off to take a look. Inside was a short note.

*Thank you for your kind words. They made a difference, and I was given a raise. Please consider me a friend any time you visit Ireland.*

When I read the signature I smiled. It was from the man at the umbrella shop.

With renewed determination to make my visit to Ireland a great one, I stepped into our room.

Once inside I kicked off my shoes, tossed down my bag, and flopped right down on the bed. As I sprawled out for what I hoped would be a relaxing nap, my hand slid under my pillow. It bumped into something hard. It felt like a book.

"My journal!" I pulled it out and stared with disbelief. Had it been under my pillow the entire time? I was sure I would have remembered putting it there.

I flipped it open and turned to the last page I'd written on. Beside it, on the next page that should have been blank, was Max's perfect handwriting.

*My Love,*

*Please don't be angry. I stumbled across this journal and I couldn't resist reading it. Once I did, I knew there were some things I needed to say before I could give it back. I wish you were comfortable talking to me face-to-face about these things, but I know that may take some time. So for now, if you'll let me, I'd like to be able to write back and forth with you in this journal.*

*If you don't like the idea, it's okay. I just want the opportunity to tell you that everything you're feeling, all the worries and doubts you experience—I experience those same things.*

*But never about you. Only about me.*

*You are the one thing in my life that I am absolutely certain about. I want to be the same for you. I understand that you've been through some things that make that difficult, but I will be here every step of the way until you can look into my eyes and be absolutely certain about my love for you.*

*I planned a special surprise for you today, and I hope you will like it. I want us to be honest about what we want from life—from each other and for our future. There is nothing that you can't tell me.*

*Love always,*
*Max*

LILLIANNA BLAKE

# CHAPTER 12

I couldn't stop the tears from forming as I put two and two together. My journal was never missing. Max had it the whole time. He'd written a sweet love note for me the night before, and I'd never even read it. If I'd only mentioned to him that I thought I'd misplaced the journal, he would have given it to me right away. Instead, I'd stressed most of the day about it and let my imagination run wild.

He was right. I needed to find my certainty in him.

As I wiped my eyes, the door to the hotel room opened and Max stepped inside. I looked up from the journal in time to see his skin grow pale.

"Oh, I didn't mean to interrupt."

"Max, please. Sit with me."

He nodded and sat down beside me on the bed. "Listen, before you say anything, I know it was an invasion of your privacy to read that. I'm sure that's what you were upset about today, and I'm sorry. It was foolish of me to write in it when it belongs to you."

"No, it wasn't foolish at all. The truth is—without

you, it's not complete. It's a journal about our relationship, and that means that it belongs to both of us. It's also not what I was upset about. I only found it now."

"You did?" He looked up at me with surprise. "Then what was bothering you today?"

I took a deep breath and remembered the last line in his note. "I thought I'd lost the journal. As you know, it has some very personal information in it about us. I was afraid that if I told you I lost it, you'd be upset with me."

"Oh, Sammy." He hugged me. "What am I going to do with you?"

"Make me breakfast in bed again?" I smiled.

"No. Well, yes—maybe, but no. This isn't something to joke about. When you're worried about something—when you're feeling stressed—I should be the first person you turn to, not the person you're afraid to talk to."

"I know. I'm going to try harder at being honest. I love your idea about writing back and forth and I hope that we can continue to do that."

"I'd really like to. I'm sorry that you thought you lost the journal, though. If I'd told you what I'd done, you wouldn't have worried all day."

"It doesn't matter now. Tomorrow we get to see the countryside, and we can continue to enjoy our time together. That's all that matters to me."

The next morning I woke up feeling lighter than I had in a long time. I hadn't realized how much it bogged me down to keep something from Max. I promised myself that I would be more open with him from now on.

I gazed at him while he slept. The subtle way his cheeks pinked up and the purse of his lips made me certain that he was a work of art, not an actual person. Then he snored and swung his hand at me in his sleep. I laughed as I realized that he'd probably sensed me staring at him.

I climbed out of bed and headed for the shower.

When I emerged from the bathroom, I didn't see Max in the room. For a moment I wondered if he'd found something better to do, but I pushed the thought away.

"Max?"

"Out here." He slid the balcony door open.

I smiled as I stepped out to find fruit and tea waiting for me. "Do you mind if we eat breakfast out here today?"

"Not at all. This is lovely. Thank you."

He pulled out a chair for me. "Something to brighten your day, since I don't think the sun is going to make it out of the clouds."

"I don't mind. I like the brooding sky. It makes me think of poetry, and romance, and epic things in general."

"You get all that from the sky?" He glanced up at it. "I wish I could see through your eyes once in a while."

"Trust me—it's a blessing and a curse."

"I imagine it could be." He picked up a piece of melon and popped it into his mouth.

"This is a perfect way to say goodbye to Dublin, Max." I picked up my cup of hot tea and took a sip.

Beyond the balcony the traffic and rush of the city created music and entertainment.

"It seemed that you liked the balcony, so I thought we should enjoy it on our last morning here."

"I'm so looking forward to exploring."

"Me too." He sipped his tea and stretched in his chair.

I couldn't help but study the way his body flexed and sprawled into a relaxed state. I hadn't lost an ounce of attraction for Max. The way he looked back at me conveyed that he hadn't lost any for me either. In that moment, I could call myself happy—in our little bubble of love and with the relaxation of not having a timeline. Although I was grateful for the success of the book, I longed for these moments when there was nothing to do but enjoy one another's company.

"Did you sleep well last night?"

"Well enough. It's a bit noisy here." He shrugged. "What about you?"

"Pretty good. Every time I woke up, I just snuggled up to you."

"I know." He smiled. "I enjoyed it."

"I suppose when we're finished here we should pack up."

"Yes, it's probably best to get out of the city in between the rush hours. Anything else you need to do while we're here in Dublin?"

"Not a thing. Now all of my time is devoted to you, Max."

"To us." He held up his cup of tea.

I held up mine and clinked it to his. "To us." I smiled as I took another sip.

It startled me how pleasurable a moment could be—without thought given to the past or to the future. I could drown in his eyes, without hesitation or a time limit. It was as intimate to me as any moment we'd ever spent in bed together.

LILLIANNA BLAKE

# CHAPTER 13

Max gazed back at me with a slight smile on his lips. It made me think he knew some wonderful secret about me.

"Your book signings are all lined up for when we get back?"

The moment shattered, I nodded. "Yes. I think Fiona has a good handle on everything."

"Great—one less thing to stress about."

"That's for sure. I want to do something special for her. She's really been so kind to me, and she's such a big fan. Any ideas?"

He gazed up at the cloudy sky for a moment then looked back at me. "Put her in your next book?"

"Good idea." I laughed.

"I'm serious. Or better yet, talk about her on the blog. I'm sure she'd enjoy that."

"That's not a bad idea. Maybe there's a way that I can work it in. But not now. Now, we're going to pack up and leave Dublin in our dust."

"Does it ever get dry enough here for there to be

dust?"

"You know what I mean." I grinned, then finished my tea.

After I cleared the cups, I headed inside to pack my things. Of course Max was already packed up. He would have packed me up too, but I'd put a stop to that early on in our marriage. I had to do some things for myself or I would feel totally useless.

Once we were ready, we headed downstairs to pick up the car. Max walked up to the counter to talk to the attendant.

When the attendant pointed out a car, Max's voice grew a bit louder.

"You couldn't have washed it?"

"Sure, if you want to pay the extra thirty dollars."

"Thirty dollars for a car wash?"

I could tell from the tone of his voice that Max's frustration had begun to escalate.

"Where are the keys?"

"Here you are sir." The man dropped the keys into Max's hand.

Max glanced over his shoulder at me.

I walked up to him with a cheerful smile. "Don't worry, honey. Whatever car it is will be just fine."

"It's this one." He led me over to it and sighed.

"This is the car you rented?" I stared at the green car. Maybe I could have figured out what make and model it was, if it weren't so covered in mud. From what I could tell it was just a green car.

"Uh, it doesn't exactly look like the picture." Max frowned. "I can get a different one, but the guy said it'll be a few hours before one is available."

"No way. This is fine. As long as it runs, right?" I flashed a smile at him.

"Ah yes, the way of the frugal Sammy."

"I'm serious. It's not just about the cost, it's about the time it will cost us. If we leave now, we'll have plenty of time to explore. If not, we'll be rushed and stressed. What does it matter what we're  driving?"

"You're right. It doesn't matter at all. Let's get going." He opened the passenger side door for me.

"Oh, I thought I was driving?"

"Ha!" He stared at me with a wide grin. "Ha, that's very funny. No."

"What are you talking about, Max? I'm a great driver."

"If you say so." He lifted an eyebrow in my direction. "Let me start out, then when I get tired you can take over."

"Max." I crossed my arms. "I can drive just fine."

"This is a different country, you know. It's not the same as driving back home."

"Like I said, I can handle it. But if you insist, I guess I'll just play with the radio."

"Great." He held the door open for me until I got in the car. Then he closed the door behind me.

I started to fiddle with the radio when he put the key in the ignition. I soon discovered that the radio was only there for decoration and didn't actually work.

"Bummer, no tunes." I sighed and glanced over at him. "I guess I'll just have to sing."

"Sounds good to me." He flashed a grin at me as we started out down the road.

I began to sing a song we both knew fairly well. He soon joined in with me.

As the wind ruffled my hair and the city disappeared behind us, Max's voice surrounded me. It was another one of those moments that should have been frozen in time as one I could live in forever.

Not long after we left the city, we were alone on the road. We rested our voices. Max gazed through the windshield.

I stared out the window at the transition from urban to countryside. The green hills enraptured me. It was more beautiful than pictures could ever convey.

After a few miles of empty road Max glanced at the clock on the dash. "Why don't we stop for a little while? You can get some pictures and we can have some lunch."

"Stop where?" I looked over the empty countryside.

"We've got a blanket, we've got food, so anywhere." He winked at me.

"Great idea!"

He pulled off to the side of the road near an open pasture.

# CHAPTER 14

I spread out my blanket on the grass while Max gathered some food from the cooler. We put together sandwiches and sipped tea out of a thermos. Max stretched out across the blanket and I rested my head against his chest to look up at the sky. The clouds were so thick and heavy that it should have been raining. Instead, they just hovered above me with the promise of rain to come. I snapped a picture with my cell phone, then turned over to snap a picture of Max. He smiled at me as I took the picture.

"You have no idea what this experience with you means to me."

"Yes, I think I do." I leaned down and kissed him.

He pulled me down beside him to continue the kiss. As our caresses grew a bit more intimate I was startled by his warm breath on my neck.

"Max, don't you know that drives me crazy?"

"What? This?" He kissed me again.

But I still felt the hot breath on the back of my neck.

"Max!" I shrieked and pulled away from him.

When I turned around I came face to face with a rather curious sheep.

Max broke out into laughter as I shrieked again and tried to climb over him to get away from the sheep.

"Relax, he's not going to hurt you."

"He was breathing on me!"

"I don't blame him." He grinned. "You're gorgeous."

"Max! Be serious." As soon as the words left my mouth I broke out into laughter as well. It was pretty funny. I flopped back on top of him and snuggled close. "I guess we have an audience now."

"A pretty large one." Max tipped his head toward the rest of the flock. "Maybe we should move along and let them have their spot back."

"You're right. They might decide they want to breathe on your neck next, and unlike some people, I don't want random sheep breathing on my spouse."

"Hey, that's not fair. I didn't allow it, I just found the beauty in it." He laughed again and helped me to my feet.

I folded up the blanket while Max packed up the leftover food. The sheep watched us the entire time. I'd never really thought about what a sheep's thoughts might be like. Did they know they'd interrupted our picnic? Did they think we'd interrupted theirs? It was pretty amusing to think about. One was so cute and fluffy that I had to reach out and pat its head.

"Oh, Sammy, I'm not sure that's a good idea." Max

closed the trunk of the car.

"It's just a sheep. They're harmless. Get a picture of me with it, please."

Max pulled out his cell phone.

I patted the sheep's head again. The sheep let out a deep sound—similar to a growl. Then all of his sheep friends let out the same low sound.

"Uh, Sammy." Max lowered his cell phone. "We need to get in the car."

I inched away from the sheep, but he continued to stare at me, as did all of his sheep friends.

"Max, I don't like the way they're looking at me!"

"Run, Sammy!" Max waved his hands at the sheep.

Their big dark eyes continued to fixate only on me. I broke into a run toward the car. As I ran, the sheep did too. I grabbed the door handle of the car and flung myself inside.

Max ran around to the driver's side and jumped in as well.

Once the doors were closed the sheep surrounded the car. They bleated loudly and rubbed against the car enough to make it rock. Max and I looked at one another and I burst into uncontrollable laughter. Max soon joined in.

He turned the car on and beeped the horn in an attempt to get the sheep to move. The stubborn animals didn't budge. Max inched the car forward just enough to warn them and finally they broke apart and fled.

"That was wild! How does something like that even happen?" I laughed so hard I could barely catch a breath.

"Only you, Sammy. I guess the sheep are fans too."

"I'm not sure. From the way they were looking at me—I'm not sure what they had in mind."

"Funny." He grinned at me and reached over to pat my knee. "You're safe now."

"No thanks to you. 'Run, Sammy!' Really, Max?

"What did you want me to do?" He chuckled. "I couldn't exactly throw crackers at them."

"You could have tried." I punched his arm playfully. "I'm just kidding. You were my hero, as usual."

"That was quite an experience. Hopefully we can get to our destination without another hiccup."

Just as Max spoke, a car barreled straight for us, blaring its horn.

"Look at this crazy fool! He's driving on the wrong side of the road!" Max turned the steering wheel hard. "Hold on, Sammy!"

# CHAPTER 15

Max drove right off the road and into the pasture filled with sheep. The sheep ran as Max slammed on the brakes.

"What a lunatic!" He blared his horn.

The sheep ran faster.

"Uh, Max." I cleared my throat and tried to keep my voice calm.

"Are you okay, Sammy? I should go hunt him down and knock him out. He could have killed us both!"

"Max, darling." I touched his arm.

"I just don't understand how someone can be that foolish. Why would he even be driving if he doesn't know which side of the road to be on?"

"Remember, we're in Ireland."

"I know that, why are you talking nonsense?" He looked over at me. "Did you hit your head or something? Are you sure that you're okay?"

"I'm fine. I promise. But I think maybe I should drive from now on."

"Why? It wasn't my fault. I saved us!"

"Max, you were the one on the wrong side of the road."

"No, I wasn't—"

"Yes, you were. Think about it."

Max stared at the road, then looked back at me. "Are you sure?"

"Yes, Max. I'm sorry. It's an easy mistake to make. Are you okay?"

"I think so. I'm not sure that the sheep are, though."

"They do look a little traumatized." I covered my mouth with my hand to avoid a giggle.

"Sammy."

"I'm sorry." I tried to keep a straight face. "I know it's not funny, but the way those sheep were running—it's just stuck in my mind."

"It's not funny. We could have been seriously hurt and—" He coughed to cover a laugh. "I'm serious."

"Oh, I know it, Max. It's not funny at all." I looked into his eyes. "But I wasn't worried for a second. You're a great driver—when you're on the right side of the road."

He broke into a grin. "Alright, alright, you're not going to let me forget this, are you?"

"Well that depends…Are you going to hand over those keys now?"

"Sure." He dropped the keys into my hand.

We switched spots and I pulled the car back onto the road. It took me a second to figure out which side I needed to be on, but then we were on our way again.

Max looked out the passenger side window as I drove.

"Max, it was just an accident. It's no big deal."

"It is a big deal. You could have been hurt."

"I wasn't. In fact, not even the sheep were hurt."

He looked over at me and grinned. "Physically, but think of the mental trauma."

"That can't be helped." I smiled at him. "They'll heal."

As we continued down the road I tried to resist teasing him about the sheep.

"Sammy, you can drive a little faster, you know."

"I think this speed is just fine."

"We do have a bit of a schedule."

"Do we?" I looked over at him. "Does it include terrorizing sheep?"

"Oh, you've been waiting to say that, haven't you?" He grinned at me.

"Don't tease me about my speed, and I won't tease you about the sheep."

"Fair enough." He patted my knee. "I suppose we'll get there sometime."

"Max!"

He laughed and looked back out the window. "This place is absolutely stunning. I don't know why anyone wouldn't want to live here."

"That's a thought."

"Hm?" He looked over at me.

"Have you ever thought of living in another country?"

"Not really. It's just not something I ever considered."

"Before we started traveling, the notion of visiting foreign countries was a dream to me. Yes, I knew there were other cultures out there, but they were so far removed from me that I didn't think much about them. Now that we've experienced some of them, I see how easily I could transition into a new country."

"I don't know. As beautiful as it's been on our travels, our home still feels like home. You know? I mean—it will feel that way once we're back." He smiled at me. "We have so many wonderful memories there. Although I do love the idea of traveling—as long as we have a home base to return to."

"Me too. That would be a lot of fun."

It wasn't much longer before we pulled into an area that began the Ring of Kerry. I parked the car near a restaurant and we both got out as fast as we could.

"Oh, it feels good to be out of that car!" I stretched my arms above my head and groaned as the muscles in my body strained and then relaxed. "I think I'm going to have to get some yoga in sometime or I'm never going to be the same."

"Yes, I'm pretty stiff too." Max glanced around and took a deep breath. "Wow, this air is clean."

"It's beautiful." I smiled as I drank in the sight of the rolling hills that rose up as if they were making every attempt to be mountains.

In some places, the sky, which had lightened up to some degree, seemed to blend with the outstretched Atlantic. I'd been to many beaches, but this was far different than any other coastline I'd ever witnessed. The air held a sense of wildness, as if it was one of the few places where nature was still allowed to be raw and untamed.

The crash of the waves drew my attention.

"Ready to find something to eat?" Max pulled me toward a small restaurant.

"Yes, I guess we'd better fill our bellies before we get started on our drive." I followed Max into the restaurant.

# CHAPTER 16

Warm scents filled the air of the dimly lit tavern.

As soon as we sat down, a waitress walked over to us. "What can I get for you both today?"

"I'd like some Irish stew." I smiled. "I've been looking forward to trying some."

"And you, sir?" She looked over at Max.

"I'll try the seafood chowder."

"Excellent, it'll just be a few minutes."

As she walked away I looked across the table at Max. "So we've already had quite a journey on the way here. I can't wait to explore the Ring of Kerry."

"Did you want to go with a tour guide?" Max was looking through a pamphlet that was left on the table.

"No, I don't think so. I'd rather just go by ourselves. We might miss something on a tour."

"True, then we can go at our own pace too."

We chatted about what we might find, and soon our food was in front of us. I lost myself in the taste of the Irish stew. It tasted like something a grandmother might serve—full of flavor and just the right amount of spices.

It wasn't spicy or overcooked, it was just perfect.

Max appeared to be just as pleased with his chowder, as he didn't say a word between bites.

When we finally came up for air Max grinned. "I think I could get used to eating this way."

"We'll have to try out some of these dishes ourselves at home. It won't be the same, but they might be tasty."

"It'll certainly be fun to try." He gestured to the waitress for the check. "So are you ready for this?"

"Absolutely. But why don't we take a walk along the beach first?"

"Sure. That sounds nice."

We followed a narrow trail down from the bluff to the water. There was only a small strip of sand between us and the waves that crashed against the shore. The power of the ocean took my breath away.

"Stay close, Sammy, I don't want you getting washed away."

I grinned and held his hand tighter. "You too. Look, there are a few shells." I bent down to pick a few up from the sand.

Max collected a few loose rocks.

"Now we have a piece of Ireland to take back with us."

"And many amazing memories."

"Yes, those too." He smiled.

The draw of the powerful waves was too much for me to ignore. I had to take a step closer. I reached down and touched the froth of the waves. The water was cold and retreated as soon as I touched it.

Max stepped up behind me. "Do you want to go for a swim?"

"Very funny, Max. I think I would turn into an ice cube."

He rubbed his hands along my shoulders and upper arms. "You're chilly now, aren't you?"

"A little." I leaned back into his chest and sighed as his arms wrapped around me.

He brushed his lips along the curve of my cheek. "I love being here with you—like this."

I nodded. "It is nice—just the two of us, with no schedules to keep."

"The tour is going to be over soon."

"I know. I'm looking forward to experiencing Thailand, though—and the rest of our stops in that part of the world. It's going to be so different than Europe, I think."

"But what about after?" Max continued to nuzzle his lips along my cheek and neck. "Where are we going after your book tour adventures?"

"I guess back home. I'll continue to work on the next book."

"We could go anywhere—do anything." He gazed out at the water and rested his chin on my shoulder. "We don't have to stop exploring just because the tour ends."

"You mean keep writing while on the road?" I

shrugged. "I guess we could. But I was kind of looking forward to settling down for a little while."

"See, that's what I'm afraid of—settling."

"What do you mean?" I tilted my head enough that I could catch the corner of his eye. For Max to say that he was afraid of anything got my attention.

"That we'll get into a rut—a routine—forget about the magic of life."

"We don't have to. We can have date night and—"

"Date night?" He cringed. "That sounds awful. Every night should be date night with us."

"You're worried that we'll fall into a slump that will strain our marriage?"

"No." He released me from his arms and gently turned me around to face him. "I'm not worried about our marriage—not at all. That's rock solid. I'm worried about us—about losing ourselves in the routine of life. I've loved every minute of this journey, and although there's still more to come, I'm starting to feel a little apprehensive about what comes next. Won't going home be a letdown? I'll be on one computer, while you'll be on the other, and we'll pass each other now and then when we go for snacks or bathroom breaks. Does that sound like a passionate life to you?"

"Not at all. I see why you'd be scared of that. But it doesn't have to be like that. We can make plans, learn new things, have adventure weekends—"

"People always say that, but it's not what happens, is

it?" He frowned. "I don't know. It's just something that I've been thinking about."

"Well, let's keep talking about it. It's important that we communicate about things like this. While I might be content to curl up and watch a movie with you, that might not be what you want. I also want to be as active as possible. It's been hard to keep up with my workout routine and healthy eating choices while we've been on tour."

"I know, but that's not exactly what I mean. I love seeing your eyes light up, Sammy—the way you're fascinated by the new things we see and experience. That's what I'm talking about. I don't want that to stop—for either of us."

"Well, we can't exactly do that forever."

"Why not?" He looked into my eyes. "Who says we can't?"

All at once it struck me that Max wanted to be sure we didn't have a traditional marriage. Maybe he was concerned that we were going to lose sight of our own personal freedoms.

"You know, Max, I don't want you to feel like we have to do everything together. If there are things that you want to do on your own, you shouldn't be afraid to try them."

"No, there are things I want to do with you. Things that I don't want to miss out on because we get caught up in the day-to-day nonsense that once controlled our lives.

When we set out on this book tour, it wasn't just your life that changed, Sammy—mine did too. I now know that there are no limits to what we can experience."

"You're right." I smiled and rested my hands against his chest. "We can go anywhere and do anything that we want." I caught his lips in a quick kiss. "Right now, I want to explore the Ring of Kerry. Are you with me?"

"Always."

He kissed me in return, then we headed back up the bluff.

# CHAPTER 17

I jangled the shells in my pocket and tried not to think about what Max's words might mean. We'd never really talked too much about whether we planned to have children, but with Max's desire for a certain lifestyle and the fact that he didn't even mention starting a family in our future, it was easy for me to assume that he didn't have any desire to go through that experience any time soon.

As we walked back toward the car Max reached his hand out for the keys.

"Oh no, I don't think so." I held on to them tightly.

"What? Why not?"

"We wouldn't want to make any more sheep suffer."

"Oh, it's going to be like that, huh?" He kissed my cheek and gave my hand a squeeze. "So you're never going to let me drive again?"

"Hm. Maybe not never—just not in Ireland."

I ran to the driver's side of the car. He chased after me and caught me before I could get the door open. I prepared to relinquish the keys, but instead he pinned me back against the car and kissed me. Every muscle in my body relaxed as warmth flooded me. The keys slipped right from my hand into his.

He grinned as he pulled away from him. "What was that you said about not in Ireland?"

"I don't think I remember anything before that kiss."

He laughed and pressed the keys back into my hand. "If you really want to drive, it's all yours."

Once we were on the road I regretted my decision to drive. There was so much to look at that it was hard to pay attention to the road. Luckily, many of the other cars were going just as slow as I was.

"Take some pictures, please, Max. I want to remember all of this."

Max spent some time snapping pictures of the sky. "Look how the sunlight filters through the thick clouds. It is really beautiful." He snapped a few more pictures.

"It's like another world." I sighed and followed the curve of the road.

After about an hour passed, I noticed a thin road that jutted off from the side of were we were driving. It was lined by thick emerald grass. Sprigs of colorful flowers blossomed up in a checkerboard pattern. It looked magical, as if fairies and nymphs might consider it their playground.

I slowed the car and glanced at Max. "Do you mind if we take a detour?"

"I don't know, Sammy, is that even a road?"

"It looks like one to me."

"The ground looks pretty soft."

"I'm sure it will be fine. Look how beautiful it is."

"Alright, let's check it out."

I steered the car onto the road. The further we traveled, the more narrow it became.

"Sammy, maybe we should turn back. I don't think this is even meant to be a road."

"Wait, do you hear that?" I leaned my head out the window and listened.

"What?" Max did the same. Then his eyes widened. "A waterfall?"

"It sounds like one, doesn't it?" I looked over at him and grinned. "We have to check it out."

"Sammy, I don't know—if we go any further we might get the car stuck."

"I won't do that. I can tell when the ground is too soft."

"If you say so."

After a few more minutes, I hit a patch of road that wasn't as solid. In fact, the tires sank right into the soft ground that I realized—too late—was actually mud.

"Uh-oh."

"Uh-oh?" Max looked over at me. "What do you mean, uh-oh?"

"I'm just going to back up a little bit." I put the car in reverse and gunned the gas.

"No, Sammy, don't!" Max spoke up too late.

I'd already dug the tires deep into the mud.

He groaned as he stepped out of the car. "You're just about to the hubcaps. There's no way we're getting the car out of this."

"I'm sorry, Max. I don't know how I could be so stupid."

He sighed as he looked across the top of the car at me. "You're not stupid, Sammy. It was a mistake. But we're not going to get the car out of this mud—not on our own, anyway. We're going to have to call for help."

I pulled out my cell phone. "Max, there's no service."

"Great. Just great." Max ran his hand back through his hair.

"It's going to be okay, we'll figure it out."

"How is this going to be okay?" Max shook his head. "I guess we'll just have to walk back to the main road and see if we can flag someone down."

"That will take forever."

"I don't know what else to do, Sammy. Do you have any other ideas?"

"Why don't we go find that waterfall?" I met his eyes.

"Sammy, be serious. We have to find our way out of here."

"I am being serious. The car is stuck. There's nothing we can do right now to change that. But that doesn't mean that we can't enjoy ourselves. We'll go take a look at the waterfall. Maybe there will be better service over there—or tourists like us. I mean, ones who didn't get stuck in the mud."

"Funny. You might be right. If we don't find anyone, we can walk back up the road."

"Sounds like a plan to me." I slipped my hand into his.

# CHAPTER 18

We made our way along the narrow trail toward the sound of the rushing water. I was determined to find it, no matter how long it took me. The further we went, the more narrow the path became.

"It's louder this way." Max pointed to some brush.

I let him take the lead as we continued far off the cleared road. The scents and textures of Ireland were something I hoped to be able to translate into words for my readers. I had the feeling it was going to be impossible. It wasn't just the scent of the blossoms, or the feel of the moisture-laden air against my skin, or the sunlight that peeked through dense clouds—it was all of it combined and anchored by the warmth of Max's hand around mine.

"Here it is, Sammy!"

The excitement in Max's voice conveyed that he'd forgotten all about the car stuck in the mud. I looked past him at a small outcropping from a rocky cliff. A gush of water rolling off the edge of the cliff created a small but beautiful waterfall that cascaded into a small pool, then wound its way through the countryside in a thin stream.

"It's gorgeous." I took a few pictures of it, then tucked my phone in my pocket. "I want to see how cold it is."

Max followed right behind me as I climbed over the brush and rocks to get close to the water.

As it tumbled down across my fingers I smiled. "It's not too cold."

"Not as cold as the ocean water." Max wiggled his fingers through the water.

"I can't resist. I have to give it a try. Will you come with me?" I stretched my hand out to him.

"Sammy. All of our clothes are back at the car. We don't have anything to change into. I don't want to walk around soaking wet."

"Where's your sense of adventure, Max? What happened to 'Let's see what the world has to offer?'"

"Where are you going with this?" He narrowed his eyes.

I stared at him for a moment and debated whether I would really follow through with my idea. Then, without another word, I began to pull off my shirt.

Max's eyes widened as I tossed it to the ground beside me. I expected him to argue, or warn me about what could happen if we were caught, or even suggest that it was too cold. Instead, he pulled his shirt off as well and tossed it next to mine. My heartbeat quickened as I realized he was going to follow my lead.

We went through the process of shedding the remainder of our clothes without a single word spoken. Then I reached for his hand again. "It won't be too cold. I promise."

He smiled as he took my hand. "I'm going to hold you to that."

I whisked him away under the rush of the waterfall. The water was actually cold—very, very cold. I didn't think I was going to be able to stand it, until I felt Max's body wrap around mine. Suddenly I wasn't as cold as I'd been just seconds before.

In the midst of an amazing setting, with the fresh icy water coursing along my skin, we explored our passion for one another—creating another memory that we would never forget.

When we emerged from the water, the cool air made me shiver.

"It's colder than it was!" Max rubbed my arms.

"Hurry up. Let's get dressed."

As we threw on our clothes the sky rumbled.

"Oh no, I think it's going to rain, Max. We have to get back to the car." I grabbed his hand and pulled him with me as I ran back in the direction of the car.

"My socks, Sammy! I forgot my socks!"

"Don't worry, you have more." I laughed as I looked back at him.

He laughed too—until we reached the car.

"Sammy, if it rains, the car is only going to get stuck

deeper in the mud."

I pulled out my cell phone and tried again to find a signal. There was not even a single bar. I tried to text Fiona to ask for suggestions, but the text would not go through. I sighed and looked over at Max.

"I think I got us into a very bad situation."

"All we can do is start walking back. We might get stuck in the rain, but I think it's better then sitting in the car. You can stay here if you want while I go to see if I can find anyone to help."

"No, that's okay. I'd rather walk with you." I took his hand in mine and we began to walk back up the road we'd driven down. Though the sky rumbled, not a drop fell.

Max tugged my hand and put a finger to his lips. "Look what's coming." He pointed to a cluster of trees.

I held my breath as I caught sight of a deer. It stared at us as if we were the strange creatures to be fascinated by. Just as I pulled out my phone to take a picture, the deer darted off into the trees.

At the same moment a loud crash of thunder caught our attention. There was no drizzle of warning. No poetic pitter-patter of raindrops for us to dance in. The rain began to pound down in one sudden deluge.

"There's no way we can walk in this. Let's run back to the car and sit it out."

I nodded. We hadn't gotten too far, so within minutes we were back inside the car.

"I'm so sorry, Max, this is all my fault."

"Don't be sorry." He stroked my cheek, wiping at the raindrops that coursed down over my skin. "I love the adventures you take me on. I wouldn't want to miss a single one of them."

# CHAPTER 19

The rain began to let up a bit as I dug out a towel from our suitcases in the back seat. I handed it to Max to dry off. Instead, he used it to dry my arms and face before using it on himself.

As we looked out through the windshield, the rain eased up even more.

"That was fast." Max laughed. "Maybe it won't make the ground much more muddy."

Once the rain eased to a drizzle we climbed back out to look at the damage. Unfortunately the heavy rain had been enough to create quite a bit more mud.

"Max, this doesn't look good."

He sighed and nodded. "I have to agree. I guess we have no choice but to walk and hope the rain is going to take a break for a while."

I frowned and looked up at the sky. The moment that I did I grabbed Max's hand.

"Look, Max!" Stretched across the sky was a clear bright rainbow. "I've seen a lot of rainbows in my life, but this one is so vivid."

"It's great, but look, Sammy, there's someone coming." He waved his hands through the air. "Hey! Over here! Over here!"

The truck had no problem driving over the soft ground as it approached us. It stopped a few feet away from the car and two men got out.

"Are you stuck?" The older man adjusted his hat.

"Yes." Max shook his head. "And we don't have any signal on our phones. Is there any chance we can use yours?"

"Sorry, don't have any cell phones." The older man chuckled. "No point out here."

"Maybe you could give us a ride?" I dug into my purse. "I have some cash."

"No need, lass, we'll get you out of here." He winked at me.

I wasn't sure what to think of his statement until the younger man walked over with a towline to hook to the car. He smiled at me. "You're not the first tourists to get stuck out here, don't worry."

Although I was very grateful for their help, I was a little disappointed that we weren't the first to discover the mystical path and the waterfall.

"Thank you so much."

"Yes, thanks." Max nodded.

As they maneuvered the car out of the mud, Max and the two men exchanged a little conversation about different areas along the Ring of Kerry to visit.

Once the car was free, Max walked back over to me. "All ready to go, when you are."

"Did you give them something for their trouble?"

"No, they didn't want any money."

We both waved to the men as the truck drove away.

"Kindness must be a way of life around here. I'm glad we're having the chance to experience it."

"Me too." Max opened the door for me and held his hand out for the keys.

"Oh, I can still drive." I started to walk around to the driver's side.

"Hm, scaring sheep or getting the car stuck in the mud again. Nope, I'm driving." He plucked the keys out of my hand and jumped into the driver's seat before I could catch him.

I laughed as I walked back to get into the passenger seat beside him.

"Fine, but make sure you drive on the right side of the road."

"I'll try." He winked at me.

As we continued along the Ring of Kerry, Max pointed out some spots that the two men had told him about. "There's so much to see here. I think we'll have to come back and explore it again."

"That's a good idea."

After a bit more exploration and picture snapping we both decided we were ready to eat.

"Let's find a place near the hotel I reserved; that way

we won't have far to go to rest," said Max.

"Brilliant."

He programmed the GPS with the address of the hotel, then began to drive away from the main road. After a few turns, however, it seems that the GPS had lost signal.

"Oh no, now what?" Max frowned and tapped the screen.

"Let me try my phone." I started to put the address in, but realized I had no Internet signal to search the maps. "I think we're on our own, Max."

"Alright, just call the hotel and they should be able to give us directions."

I dialed the number and after several rings a woman answered. "Hold please!"

"Uh, wait, I—"

I was already on hold. I waited while Max tried to guess which direction we should go. The day gave way to evening, which made it even harder to read the road signs. I was still on hold. I decided to hang up and call back.

Within two rings the same woman answered. "Hold please!"

"Wait! Don't put me on hold!"

The elevator music indicated that I was too late. I sighed and looked over at Max. "No one is answering."

"We have to keep trying. What else can we do? I guess we could stop somewhere and ask for directions."

"Do we even know where we are right now?"

"Honestly, no. But I am getting tired."

"Me too." I grabbed some snacks from our luggage and shared them with him. "Let's just eat this and see if we can find another place to stay."

"Alright, I guess we can do that."

He began to drive up and down several roads. The further we got, the more the roads were spaced apart. Soon we ended up on a long winding road that ran along the ocean. In the twilight the entire world seemed to glow.

"Look, Max, there's a place to stay." I pointed to a small sign that hung by the road.

"It doesn't look very big."

"It's a bed and breakfast. It'll be fun."

"I don't know, Sammy, we don't know anything about the place. The hotel I reserved got great reviews."

"But it's here. Do you really want to keep driving and trying to find this hotel?"

"No." He sighed.

"I could drive, but you know, there was that getting stuck in the mud incident..."

"Good point. I guess we can give it a shot. If it's awful, we don't have to stay."

# CHAPTER 20

Max turned into the driveway and parked a small distance from the door. There was a light drizzle but nothing that we couldn't walk in.

I made my way to the door and knocked. A moment later a woman dressed from head to toe in green opened the door.

"Hello! Hello! Hello! Do you need a place to stay?"

I took a step back, blown away by the magnitude of her voice.

Max put his hand on my back and smiled. "Yes, we do. Do you have any rooms available?"

"Yes. There's just the one." She laughed. "I know that seems silly, but I take very good care of the room. I'm sure that you will love it. Oh, and I'm Claire, by the way—Claire O'Malley. Come in, please!"

She smiled so brightly that I couldn't even consider not going inside. She was so eager, and how bad could the room be? At least we wouldn't have any noisy neighbors to deal with.

I glanced at Max. He nodded, though his eyes were a

bit wide. We followed her inside the house and turned the corner right away.

"It's just in here. Now, you're welcome to stay until one, but I serve breakfast at seven. Most people do like to be on their way to see the sights. I'm sorry, but I don't offer lunch."

"Breakfast will be fine." I smiled.

"Seven?" Max rubbed the back of his neck. "Don't you think that's a little early?"

"Don't worry, Max, I'll save you some."

"I'm afraid I don't allow food in the room." She cringed. "The little men don't like it."

"The little men—"

"Don't ask, Max, we need some rest, right?" I smiled at him.

"Okay, sure. How much?"

"Let me just get my ledger." The woman hurried away.

"Sammy, are you sure you want to stay here?"

"As long as I'm with you, it'll be perfect."

"Alright." Max released a heavy breath and then pulled out his wallet. He paid the bill, then the woman smiled and patted his hand.

"Good luck to you, son. I'm sure you'll enjoy the room."

"Thank you. We're both just ready to rest."

"Understood. I will see you in the morning." She disappeared down the hallway.

I opened the door of the bedroom and noticed right away that it smelled minty. I flicked on the light switch and gasped. "I think I found the little men."

"Hm?" Max poked his head in as well and laughed. "Wow, this is quite a collection."

There were shelves from floor to ceiling, each one covered with small leprechaun figures. Some were even stacked on the dresser and along the windowsill.

"I think she has a fondness for leprechauns." I sat down on the end of the bed, which was covered in a thick blanket. "It could be worse."

"You're right, it could be." Max sprawled out on the bed and yawned. "Come snuggle with me. I can't fall asleep if you don't."

"Alright, let me just brush my teeth." I opened the door to the bathroom and braced myself for more leprechauns. Instead, there was only a toilet and sink. No shower, no bathtub. I cringed as I realized that maybe we should have tried harder to find our reserved hotel.

When I returned from the bathroom Max already had the lights out. I crawled into bed beside him and snuggled close. I took a deep breath and prepared to indulge in a great night of sleep.

However, just as I was about to close my eyes, I noticed a leprechaun on the shelf beside the bed. He stared at me with wide beady black eyes. My heart skipped a beat. Now, I know there's no reason to be afraid of a statue. But there were so many of them. And they all appeared to be staring at me.

I snuggled closer to Max and closed my eyes. I was sure that if I blocked them out everything would be fine. When I buried my head into his shoulder, Max snorted in his sleep. I cringed and hoped that I hadn't woken him up. When I opened my eyes again, that leprechaun was still there, waiting to greet me. I could barely stand the sight of it. The shadow-filled room created strange patterns on his green clothes.

I closed my eyes tighter and tried to block out the thought of those eyes staring at me. After several more minutes, my eyes opened again. There was the leprechaun—and one of his friends—and another. I sat up and stared back. A random light outside the window flickered and it made the leprechaun look as if he winked at me. That was it, I was sure I would never sleep again.

"Sammy?" Max shifted in the bed and turned to look at me. "What's wrong? Aren't you tired?"

"So tired." I hung my head and sighed. "But I can't sleep."

"Why not? Are you nervous about tomorrow? Or the book signing?" He sat up and looked at me. "Do you need a massage?"

"No, it's none of that." I smiled at him, then gritted my teeth. "I'll fall asleep eventually."

"Sammy, tell me. Are you upset about something?" He brushed the hair from my eyes.

"I can't tell you, Max, it's ridiculous."

"Nothing you say is ridiculous."

"Ha. Okay." I took a deep breath, then looked over at the leprechauns. "It's the little men—they're staring at me."

Max followed my line of sight. I noticed his dimples in his cheeks as he tried to hold back a smile.

"See, I told you, it's ridiculous."

"Actually, now that you pointed it out, I'm not sure if I can sleep either."

I stood up from the bed and walked over to one of the shelves. "Maybe if we just turn them around."

"There has to be a thousand of them."

"Do you want to sleep or not?" I raised an eyebrow at him.

"Alright." Max jumped up and together we began to turn every leprechaun in the room around to face the wall. One by one their creepy little eyes looked away from me.

By the time we were done, I was so exhausted that I collapsed onto the bed.

Max stood beside it, and stared down at me. I could feel his eyes traveling my body. I bit into my bottom lip and savored the sensation. At one time in my life I'd been petrified to have anyone look at me. Now, at least with Max, I craved that attention. I sensed that there was no judgment, only adoration from him.

He crawled onto the bed beside me and kissed my shoulder. "Do you think you can sleep now?"

"That depends."

"On what?" He looked into my eyes.

"On whether you're going to keep staring at me like that."

He grinned. "Want me to face the wall?"

"No." I pulled him close to me and curled my body around his. "I want you right here, just where you are."

He kissed my forehead and closed his eyes. It was a very tender moment—until Max started to snore. Then I wriggled away and found my pillow. Within a few minutes I knew I'd be sound asleep.

# CHAPTER 21

I woke up early the next morning. Since there was still about an hour before breakfast would be served, I took the time to turn all the leprechauns back around. I didn't want to offend Claire, who'd obviously gone to so much trouble to decorate the room.

In the quiet, I spread my yoga mat on the floor and stretched out on top of it. As I began to shift into position, I caught sight of the leprechauns staring at me again.

"Oh, you guys want a show?" I shifted into the next position. My muscles began to relax. My mind began to shift as well—into a state of peace. The stares of the leprechauns no longer bothered me.

The more I moved and stretched, the deeper I sank into a calm space. It was needed after the hurry of travel and the anxiety of losing the journal. As I moved into the last position, there was a loud knock on the door. I toppled right over onto my side.

"Just a minute." I glanced over at Max, who still

snored soundly from the bed.

I opened the door. Claire, dressed all in green again—this time in a long green dress—smiled at me as she held a tray out.

"Breakfast!"

"Oh thank you. I'm afraid my husband is still sleeping."

"Then you should join me. I have a beautiful patio set. Very comfortable. Will you join me?"

I hesitated. I didn't really want to have breakfast with the strange woman, but I also didn't want to wake Max, who deserved his sleep.

"Thank you, I will."

I followed her down a long hallway to a sliding glass door. Her patio set looked as if it had been there for a few decades, but I didn't care about that. When I sat down on the cushion it crackled.

"Isn't it great?" She smiled. "And look at the view!"

I glanced in the direction she pointed. There were a few trees on the hillside and some lush grass. It was pretty to look at but not as spectacular as the Atlantic views had been.

"You have a lovely home."

"Thank you. I've been very lucky. Maybe it's because of all of my little men."

"Maybe." I nodded. "I admired your collection."

"Some people find it a little strange, but I've been collecting them since I was a little girl. I know that leprechauns are just a story, but I've always been fascinated by them. The whole idea of a magical, mystical creature and the potential for very good luck—it's just too fantastic to resist. Do you believe?"

"In leprechauns?" I took a bite of the large plate of sausage she'd served me.

"No, not really in leprechauns, but in magic—in things being unexpected and unpredictable?"

I smiled as I thought about the ups and downs of our visit to Ireland so far. "Yes, I think I do."

"Isn't life so much better when you believe? I had this friend once—she told me that I needed to get rid of all my leprechauns. She said there was no magic to life and I needed to come down to earth. Well, I didn't tell her she was wrong, but I did tell her that if that was the earth she lived on, then I would be just fine in my outer space."

"I understand what you're saying. If life doesn't have that magical quality, what's the point?"

"I knew that we were kindred spirits the first time I saw you. So I'm a little goofy—oh, well. What harm does that do to anyone?"

"None at all. This breakfast is delicious, by the way."

"Try the blood pudding. It's very good."

I took a bite and tried to smile after putting it into my mouth. "Mm. Very good."

"So, are you going to the Blarney Stone?"

"I hadn't really thought about it."

"You need to go—trust me. No one should visit

Ireland without kissing the Blarney Stone. When will you have another chance to? It's a magical experience."

"I'll definitely think about it."

"Great. Now, I know I said no food in the room, but I have a plate in the oven for your husband when he wakes up. He's not an early riser, hm?"

"We've had a rough few days without much sleep."

"Feel free to heat it up for him when he wakes up." She patted my hand.

"Thank you. That's very kind of you."

# CHAPTER 22

After we finished our breakfast, I helped Claire to clear the table. Then I headed back to the room to check on Max. He was just waking up.

"There you are. Did you have breakfast already?"

"Yes, we just finished. There's some food saved for you, though."

"How did breakfast go?"

"Surprisingly well. Claire's a very sweet woman."

"It must have been a very interesting conversation."

"Actually it was. The best part was that she suggested that we must go to kiss the Blarney Stone."

"Hm. Isn't that a rock or something?"

"A very large rock, yes."

"Why would I want to kiss a rock?"

"Max, you're not supposed to ask why. You just do it."

"If I'm going to be kissing anyone other than you, I'm definitely asking questions."

"Any *thing* Max, not anyone."

"Okay, either way, I'd like an explanation."

"Let's just give it a try. What could it hurt?"

"I happen to know that in order to kiss the Blarney Stone, you have to bend almost all the way over and hang. I mean, that's some work involved, don't you think?"

"I just did yoga this morning. I'll be fine. Plus, I can practice. See?" I bent over as far as I could.

As I began to lose my balance, I steadied myself with the dresser. In the process a few of the leprechauns tumbled right off the top and struck me in the face and chest. "Ouch!"

"See what kissing leads to?" Max guided me back to my feet.

"They didn't break, did they?" I scooped the leprechauns up from the floor and set them back on the dresser.

"I see you've grown fond of the leprechauns."

"Maybe I've grown fond of the woman who collected them, or just the idea behind them. No matter what, I don't want them to be broken."

"They look just fine. But you could kiss them to make it better."

"You are so very funny. You know, I never realized just how funny you are."

"Funny, hm?" He grabbed me around the waist and pulled me close. "Is it wrong to be jealous of a rock?"

"I don't know about wrong, but there might be some

psychotherapy needed." I laughed as I gazed into his eyes. "You're not jealous, you're just afraid I'm going to fall."

"Ahem." He tilted his head toward the leprechauns. "I think they can say firsthand that falls do happen."

"Don't worry." I kissed him. "I'm not worried."

After Max ate the breakfast that had been saved for him, we left the bed and breakfast and drove in the direction of the Blarney Stone.

Along the way, we stopped at several places. Each time I got out of the car I practiced a back bend to get ready for what was ahead. If Max was embarrassed by my antics he didn't mention it, though he did always pause to watch.

At our last stop before the Blarney Stone I tried to bend even farther. As I started to rise back up, Max surprised me with a kiss. I was so startled that I lost my balance and ended up tumbling backwards on top of him.

Max laughed from underneath me. "See, I told you so."

"I don't think the Blarney Stone is going to kiss back!" I laughed as I grabbed his hand and helped him to his feet. "I'll be just fine, Max, I promise. The question is, are you okay?"

"I'm fine." He brushed off his pants and met my eyes. "I've been tackled by you before."

"True. And likely will be again."

"If my luck holds out." He swung his arm around my waist and pressed my body to his. "Still, I'm a little jealous of that rock."

"Don't be." I kissed him then looked into his eyes. "You're the only one I ever want to kiss."

"Other than a big slab of stone."

"Yes—well, other than that." I nodded. "But just once, I promise."

"I suppose I will allow it."

"Hm, I don't remember asking permission." I smirked.

"I wasn't giving permission, I was giving up." He laughed.

As we walked into a pub to have lunch I couldn't stop smiling. As beautiful as Ireland was, the fun I was sharing with Max was what meant the most to me. We shared a quick lunch, then were back on the road.

By the time we arrived at Blarney Castle, there was quite a crowd. The longer we waited in line, the more nervous I became. Would I really be able to pull this off?

Max rubbed my shoulders as we got to the front of the line. "There it is—my rival for your love." He scowled.

"Funny." I laughed but my heart wasn't in it.

I watched as the person in front of me bent all the way over backward and placed a kiss on the stone. Now that I saw it in person, it actually seemed impossible.

"Max, never mind. I can't do this. Let's just go." I grabbed his hand and started to leave the line.

He stood like stone himself and held on to my hand.

"No, I'm sorry. I can't let you do that, Sammy. I know this is something that you want to do. So you should at least give it a shot."

"But all of these people are watching. What if I make a fool of myself?"

He shrugged and glanced over his shoulder at the crowd. "What do you care what these people think of you?"

Max's question was a reminder to me. I couldn't base my decisions on fear of judgment. He was right. If I left Ireland without kissing the Blarney Stone, I would definitely regret it.

# CHAPTER 23

I took a few steps forward, thought about changing my mind, then forced myself to keep going. Kissing the Blarney Stone was a folklore tradition, but it meant a lot to me. Maybe it would help me with inspiration for my next book.

I walked up to the man beside the stone and looked into his eyes.

"This is my first time."

"Don't worry, lass, I won't drop you." He winked at me.

Somehow I didn't feel reassured. I crouched down and reached back to grab the bars.

The man grabbed my waist and hips, which was enough to set off every insecurity within me.

"You can do it, Sammy, I'm right here." Max's voice drifted down to me as I tightened my hands on the bars.

"Go further now, go further down." The man who held me gave me a little push.

As all the blood rushed to my head I wondered what had possessed me to do something like this.

Still, he prompted me to go down further. I was about to give up and demand to be pulled back in, but then I felt it—the smooth cool surface of the stone against my lips. I'd done it. A surge of pride washed over me.

I kissed the stone, then started to make my way back up. As I did so, I found that I seemed to have worked myself into a position that made getting back up impossible. In fact, I could barely wiggle at all.

"Come on back up, lass." The man gave my hips a tug.

"I'm trying." I winced. "There isn't enough room."

"Work with me here, I can't do it all on my own." He tugged again.

Only then did I realize that I wasn't just stuck, I was practically wedged. Maybe the man had urged me to go too far down, but whatever the cause, it didn't matter. I wasn't budging.

"Max? Are you still there?"

"I'm here, Sammy."

The man grunted and tugged at my body.

I wriggled again. "Max, I think I'm stuck."

"Hold on, I'll get you out." He gripped my hips along with the man and started to tug, but as he did he laughed.

I stared at him with horror as he laughed even louder. "Max! Get me out of here!"

"I'm trying, just give me a second." He tried to hold back his laughter but his whole body trembled.

I rolled my eyes. I could tell from the noise that quite

a crowd had gathered to see my predicament.

Max finally gave me a good hard pull, but my body didn't budge.

It occurred to me that I might have to be hoisted out by a crane of some kind.

"I'm stuck, Max. I don't think you can get me out. I can't believe this is happening."

"Don't worry, Sammy, I'm going to get you out."

"Here, lad, let me help you with that." I heard a strange voice as someone stepped up beside Max. Soon a stranger's hands were on my hips. I was horrified but hopeful that he would be able to get me out. He tugged hard and I slid up about an inch. "We're going to need some more help."

As the commotion increased I gathered from snippets of conversation that the entire crowd planned to work together to get me free. I couldn't believe that I'd let myself get into such a ridiculous situation.

Minutes later I was free and wrapped in Max's arms. The crowd around us cheered, but I buried my face in Max's shoulder. I couldn't look anyone in the eye.

"Sammy, don't be embarrassed. Look how many people were here to help you." Max whispered in my ear.

I peeked up above his shoulder and saw a crowd of about thirty people. All of them looked at me expectantly.

I pulled away from Max and smiled. "Thank you, everyone!"

The crowd applauded again and then the line

reformed and people continued to kiss the Blarney Stone.

"Max, this is awful."

"It's not as bad as you think."

"No, you're right. It's worse!" I sighed.

"It's really not. It was an experience, right?" He smiled.

I wanted to have that positive outlook, but there was a woman staring at me so hard that I was sure she wanted to point and laugh. But maybe that was the positive side of it. Maybe the idea that the story could bring amusement to others was enough reason to be grateful for it.

"Yes, quite an experience. I think I have to have a record of this for my blog. Will you take a picture of me, Max?"

"Of course I will. Anyone want to join in?" Max glanced over at the people in line. "Just a memory for her blog."

The woman who'd been staring at me walked over to us along with a few other people who had helped to pull me out. They collected around me and squeezed in tight.

After Max took a few pictures everyone began to break apart. However, the one woman lingered right beside me.

"Can I ask what the blog is that he was referring to?"

I told her about my book and the Single Wide Female blog. The instant I mentioned who I was, her eyes lit up.

"Oh, I'm such a big fan. In fact, my book club has

read your book. Oh, I don't suppose you would have any free time to meet them, would you? We're meeting tonight, actually."

"I'm not sure. We are on a bit of a schedule." I glanced over at Max. "I'm not sure that we have anything planned for this evening, though."

"If you could come, it would be amazing. Several of the people in the book group are fans, and I'm sure they would so enjoy meeting you. I know that it's asking a lot, but I hope that you'll consider it."

"Let me just check with my husband and see if we're free, then I'll let you know."

When I walked over to Max he was just finishing a conversation with one of the men that had helped to pull me out.

"Max, what do you think about doing a little meet-and-greet at a local book club tonight?"

"Oh, I don't know. It's not on the schedule."

"No, it isn't, but it wouldn't take long, and it would make one of my readers very happy."

"What about Fiona? Do you think she would mind?"

"I doubt it. I don't think anyone would even know about it. But I could send her an e-mail to check."

He met my eyes. "You know we can't go to every fan's book club."

"Yes, I know that, but we can go to just this one, can't we?"

"I suppose we could, if it's what you want to do."

"It is. I'm really excited about it."

"Okay, then let's do it." He shrugged and looked over at the woman I'd met. "I'm sure it'll be a great experience for all of us."

"Great! I'll let her know."

# CHAPTER 24

As I walked back over to the woman, my heart swelled with happiness. This was the kind of thing that I liked—directly connecting with my readers, instead of having a podium or a computer screen between us. I just hoped that I would be able to live up to her expectations.

"We can certainly attend tonight. If you want to give me the address and the time, we'll be there."

"Wow, I can't believe this. Thank you so much. I can't wait to tell everyone. You're going to have a great time. I promise. My name is Shauna, by the way, and I can't wait to introduce you to everyone."

"I'm looking forward to it, Shauna. I'm glad you asked." I jotted down the time and address on my phone, then waved to her as I walked away.

Max grinned at me as I joined him near the car. "So, do I get to say it now?"

I stared at him. "Say what?"

"Something about I told you so." His grin spread so far that his dimples sunk deep into his cheeks.

"Okay, but only once, and then you have to drop it for the rest of the trip."

"I think I can promise you that." He opened the door for me. "I am definitely driving."

"Yes, I think that might be a good idea." I rubbed my lower back. "That bend was a bit more strenuous than the ones I'd been practicing."

"But the important question is, how was the kiss?" He leaned into the car to kiss my cheek. "Not better than mine, I hope?"

"Not even close." I kissed him just before he closed the door.


After a leisurely dinner we headed to Shauna's house.

"I'm excited to have the chance to dine with a real Irish family."

"It will be nice to see how the locals actually live and eat." Max steered the car down a long road toward the address. "Let's not stay too long, though. I want to be sure we have some time together tonight."

"Okay." I glanced over at him. "Any particular reason?"

"Now that I know where the hotel is, I'd like to get there early enough for us to enjoy some time in the hot tub."

"You are full of great ideas, Max."

"I know." He grinned.

When we parked in front of the modest house I was a little nervous. I had become accustomed to the more formal book signings with a start and finish. What would this be? Would they want to ask me lots of questions? Would they want me to read from one of their books? I was going in blind and that was new to me.

Max took my hand as we walked up to the door. "If anything seems off, just tap your cheek and I'll get you right out of here."

"Thanks, Max. I'm sure everything will be fine." I knocked on the door.

Almost immediately the door swung open and I was greeted by Shauna's eager smile.

"You see! I told you that she would come!" She stepped back to reveal about ten people clustered behind her. There were both men and women, and they ranged in age from teens to one woman who appeared to be in her sixties or seventies.

"Hi, everyone. Thank you for inviting me."

"It's really you." One of the men shook his head. "Shauna said she met you, but she tells stories sometimes."

"Douglas, I do not. You just don't believe me. That doesn't mean I'm lying."

"Okay, Shauna, tell us about the woman with the wagon full of leprechauns again?"

"I saw her!" She stamped her foot and laughed.

"Sure you did." The rest of the group laughed right

along with Douglas.

I opened my mouth to point out that the story might be true but before I could speak the older woman stepped forward.

"Douglas, don't tease Shauna. There is nothing wrong with an imaginative mind. Isn't that right, Samantha?" She smiled at me.

"Yes, I think so. Where would I be without a little imagination?" I smiled in return. I felt an instant closeness to this woman. Maybe it was because I'd never really known my grandmother, or maybe we had some unknown things in common, but I was certain that although I'd never met her, I already knew her.

"I'm Aislin. Welcome to our group." She offered me her hand.

The warmth captured in her long thin fingers was something I'd never experienced before. It rippled through me, as comforting as a warm hug.

"It's a pleasure to meet you, Aislin."

"We have a little area set up for you in here. I know it's a bit cramped, but—well, there's tea!" Shauna smiled and led me toward a small living room. As many chairs as possible were crammed into the small space.

# CHAPTER 25

As we settled in chairs, I noticed a sound coming from another room in the house.

Shauna seemed to notice my gaze as she walked over to me. "I'm sorry. A few of our kids are in the other room. They won't be any trouble though."

"Oh, you don't have to worry about me. I don't mind kids at all. They're welcome to join us if you want them to."

"I'm sure they'll be out here soon enough." Shauna laughed. "They can't stay out of things for too long." She settled into a chair.

After drinks and snacks were passed around, all the focus turned to me.

"Shauna mentioned that you've all read my book. So if you have any questions please feel free to ask."

"Honestly, I don't have any questions about the book, but I do have a ton about you." Aislin sat forward in her chair. "Can we ask you anything we want?"

"Uh, sure." I glanced at Max who shook his head

slightly. "Within reason, of course."

"Wonderful. When did you first know that you would be a writer?"

"I can't honestly say that there was a moment that I made that decision. It's more like writing chose me. There was never a time that I didn't have a story running through my mind. One day I just started to write it down on paper."

"What are your plans after the book tour?" Shauna waved her hand in the air.

"We're not sure just yet. That's still up in the air."

As the women asked a few more questions I glanced over at Max. He seemed engrossed in the question and answer portion. I fielded a few more questions about my next book, then picked up my drink. In that moment, three children barreled right through the living room and knocked the drink out of my hand. I braced myself for an explosion, but as I stared into their inquisitive, apologetic eyes, I didn't feel any anger at all.

Their mother soon arrived with a moist rag in hand. The mess was cleaned up and not a single tear was shed. I patted my knee and the littlest boy crawled up into my lap.

"I bet you have a very imaginative mind, don't you?"

"Aye." His eyes sparkled as they looked into mine.

"Isn't he adorable, Max?" I looked over at him in time to see him lunge away from the directed swing of a toddler's foot.

He shook his head as he looked over at me. While I basked in the glow of a curious child's attention, he looked as if he'd rather be anywhere else on earth.

As the evening wound down I drew my attention away from the children and focused it back on Shauna. She was the mother to two of the boys as well as an older girl. When they piled on top of her I saw the gleam in her eye. She teased them and poked at their bellies. She smothered them in kisses one moment and commanded their attention the next. She did it all with such ease.

I wondered what it was that transformed a woman into a mother. I knew that it wasn't just pregnancy and childbirth—that wasn't what created the confidence and natural instinct that I could see in Shauna. I'd met a few mothers that didn't have either of those things. So what secret did she discover that made her cuddle her child close, even when there was an entire world of worry to focus on?

Max sat down beside me and I slipped my hand into his. I savored the experience.

"Are you about ready? It's a little chaotic in here." He spoke his words soft enough that he wouldn't offend anyone, but those words cut into me. While I sat there marveling over the beauty of the parent-child relationship, Max seemed to be barely tolerating it at best.

"Sure, I guess." I nodded and started to stand up.

"Wait!" Shauna grinned. "I know you're busy—if you can't stay, that's fine—but there is a bit more to our book club."

"Oh?" I looked between the members of the group. "What is it?"

"Dancing!" Aislin pushed a button on a radio and in moments Irish music flooded the house.

The children dropped whatever they were doing and began to dance. I couldn't resist following suit. That sense of freedom, the lack of care about what others thought, the purity of the way they moved their bodies to the music was enough to make me long for that twilight stage. It was a time I couldn't remember and one day they wouldn't, either—a time when everything was magical and nothing was impossible.

As everyone began to dance, I reached for Max's hand.

He hesitated. "Sammy, there's not much room in here. Some of these people have been drinking."

"Max, it's just a little fun. Won't you dance with me?"

"I suppose." He sighed as I pulled him to the center of the room.

Within a few minutes of dancing he began to enjoy himself. The children laughed, their parents sang, and Max held me so close that I forgot all about his demeanor toward the children.

As the children began to grow sleepy, the music was turned down and our hostess brought out the Guinness. Max declined the drink but helped to carry the children off to bed.

As we gathered our things and headed for the door Aislin caught my arm.

"Might I ask for just one more moment?"

"Sure." I smiled.

"Over here—where's it's quiet." She gestured to a small hallway.

# CHAPTER 26

I followed Aislin into the hallway, curious about what she might want to say.

"I noticed your way with the children. You don't have any of your own yet?"

"No, not yet."

"I never had children myself. I could, but I didn't think I wanted any, and then when I might have changed my mind, it was too late. My husband gave me this ring." She opened her hand to reveal a Claddagh ring. "Tradition says it should be handed down to our daughter, but of course we didn't have any. I know this may seem strange to you, but I would like to hand it down to you."

"I couldn't possibly accept."

"I wish you would. No, you're not my daughter, but you've inspired women all around the world. One day you'll have a daughter of your own to hand it down to. Or if you have a son, you can give it to his wife. It would mean so much to me if you would accept it. It's really just a trinket, but I have no one to give it to." She pressed the ring into my hand and closed my fingers over it. "I would like you to have it."

"Thank you." The words came out as a whisper. I was so touched that she'd given me the ring that it didn't seem right to protest. "I will take very good care of it."

"I'm sure that you will, Samantha. Keep writing. You're going to touch more hearts than you could ever realize."

After I hugged Aislin goodbye I met Max out by the car. Once we were in the car I opened my hand to reveal the ring with tears in my eyes.

"Isn't it beautiful?"

"Yes, it is. Where did you get it?"

"Aislin gave it to me. She handed it down to me. She asked me to give it to my daughter one day."

"Your daughter?" He laughed.

His laughter stung. I sat back and stared through the windshield.

Max seemed to notice my silence and looked over at me as he drove. "Sammy, did I say something wrong?"

"Why would you laugh about that?"

"About what? You having a daughter?"

"Yes."

He returned his gaze to the road. "Oh, I just thought you were joking."

"Max, you don't want to have kids, do you?"

He slowed the car and looked over at me again. "I didn't think either of us did, really. I mean, maybe one day…" He wiped a hand across his mouth and then sped up the car a little more. "But we have been pretty busy with your work schedule. It's hard to imagine doing that all with kids around." He glanced over at me.

"Right."

"Sammy, can we talk about this back at the hotel?"

"I guess there's no need to. You don't want to have children."

"Now wait, that's not true. I just don't think that this is the time to think about that. I mean things are pretty up in the air."

"You wouldn't want to lose any of your freedom."

He pulled into the parking lot of the hotel and turned the car off. Then he shifted so that he could look directly at me.

"Don't put words in my mouth, Sammy. You just sort of sprung this on me. I'm still sorting through it. It's not like you've been talking about kids, either."

"No, I haven't really talked about it, but I think a part of me just assumed it came with the package."

"Marriage and kids?"

"I mean, if we both wanted them, of course. Max," I sighed. "I would never want you to do anything that you didn't want to do."

"Let's just get through the book tour, then we'll talk about it, alright?"

I nodded but had to bite into my bottom lip to hold back a flurry of words. I didn't want to get through anything, I wanted to live life to its fullest.

After we checked into the hotel Max took a shower while I found a safe spot to store the ring. I wondered if I should give it back to Aislin. If I wouldn't ever have children, shouldn't it go to someone else?

All at once it occurred to me that the abstract notion of being a mother, which had never really drawn my attention before, was now a deep urge. There was no question in my mind any more that I wanted kids. Unfortunately, I suspected that there was no question in Max's mind that he didn't.

We spent the next two days exploring more of the countryside. Though we had ample time to discuss it, the topic of having children never came up again.

As we prepared to head back to Dublin, I tucked the ring into my purse. I planned to keep it. If I met a mother, I could give it to her. To my complete surprise it made my eyes mist to think that it would never be me.

Max stuck his head into the hotel room. "Ready?"

"Yes. I have everything." I smiled at him. He was an amazing man and I was lucky to have him. I wasn't going to let something like this come between us, either. I put the thought of having children out of my head and settled in for the journey back to Dublin.

Thick silence settled in the car between us. It wasn't awkward but it was heavy.

Max stopped for gas and while we stretched our legs I checked my e-mail on my phone.

"I just got an e-mail from my contact in Thailand." I smiled as I showed him the e-mail on my phone.

"Wow, is that her? She looks so young." Max studied the picture embedded in the e-mail. I hadn't really noticed it until he'd pointed it out. She was petite and perfect, with bright brown eyes and sweetheart lips. My heart skipped. In general, women in Thailand were very small. I would likely appear a giant to them.

"She's very pretty." I studied the picture a little longer.

"Thailand is going to be a big change. No Blarney Stone to kiss."

"Hopefully not." I laughed and tucked my phone away.

A laugh could break the tension within me, but it couldn't erase the insecurity that had cropped up at the thought of being surrounded by petite women. An image of me as Godzilla, stomping my way through a pristine city, with petite women running from me in all directions, flashed through my mind. I dismissed it the moment it did, but my cheeks still burned.

"It's going to be great." Max wrapped his arms around me and kissed my cheek. "I love getting to see all of these places with you."

"Me too." I lowered my eyes.

"Sammy? Is something wrong?"

"No. I think I'm just nervous about the book signing. Would it be okay if we stayed at the hotel until it's time to go?"

"Sure, of course. I'll order dinner."

"You're so good to me, Max."

"You deserve it, Sammy." He held my gaze. "Never forget that."

# CHAPTER 27

When we left for the book signing my stomach was in knots. I wasn't nervous about the event, but about whether I could be open and honest with Max about the sadness that I was suddenly feeling.

As soon as I walked in the door Fiona was there to greet me.

"I saw the picture of your smooch at the Blarney Stone—and heard the story!" She laughed as she slapped my shoulder. "I wish I'd been there to see it."

"Yes, it was a little embarrassing." I cringed.

"And great marketing. I've got people calling to find out about you. Are you ready for tonight?"

"Yes, I think I am."

We discussed the flow of the night, then she invited Max and me to go out after the book signing. I thought it might be a good idea for us both to have a little more fun.

"Sounds lovely."

"I know a great place."

"I'm sure you do." I grinned at her and walked

toward the podium.

The question and answer session went very smoothly. Then I read a portion of the book and settled at the table to sign autographs. As nice as it was to meet more of my readers, it was nothing like being at Shauna's. I missed the chaos, the noise, the assortment of opinions, and the laughter.

As the book signing came to a close Fiona walked over to me.

"What a great night. If tomorrow night is this good, then I have to say that this leg of your tour has been very successful."

"I think so too, thanks to you, Fiona. You did a great job putting this together."

"Tell me that over some drinks, hm? Now where's that handsome hubby of yours?"

I laughed and pointed to Max near the back of the room.

As Fiona walked off to introduce herself, I noticed that one of the women who had attended the book signing had a baby in a sling across her chest. My heart softened. Never before had I felt such a pull, but there it was.

Max and Fiona walked back toward me and I shifted my attention from the baby.

"Ready for a night you won't forget?" Fiona smiled.

"Absolutely." I wrapped my arm around Max's and leaned close to him.

He responded with a kiss to my forehead. As much as I wanted that experience of being a mother, I wouldn't give up the experience of Max with his arms around me.

We traveled to a small club and in no time had joined Fiona on the dance floor.

"Now listen, you two, don't strain anything trying to keep up with me. I've got a bit more experience than the two of you.

Max and I exchanged a grin, then began to dance. It wasn't long before we showed off the skills we'd learned in Shauna's living room.

"Wow, I'm impressed. May I cut in?" Fiona tapped my shoulder.

"Is it okay with you, Max?" I met his eyes.

"Sure." Max smiled at Fiona as she took his hand.

I stood back and watched him dance with Fiona. It impressed me that he treated her with such care. I admired him in ways that I would never be able to fully define. There were no other options for me, only Max. Just as he accepted me and all my strange ways, I knew that I needed to accept him, even if he didn't ever want to have children.

When Fiona left his side he walked straight over to me. I thought he would pull me back onto the dance floor. Instead he stroked his hands across my cheeks and looked into my eyes.

"Something's bothering you. What's going on?"

"It's nothing, really." I smiled at him.

"Sammy. I thought we agreed that we were going to be open and honest with each other."

"We did." I kissed his cheek. "I'm fine."

"Look, if you can't talk to me about it, then just write about it in our journal. Alright? Get it out. Put some words to that look in your eyes, because I want to know every part of you and everything that might be weighing on your mind. Will you do that for me?"

"Yes." I hugged him. "Yes, I will."

We spun around the dance floor a few more times before we said goodbye to Fiona. It seemed to me that my entire journey through Ireland had gone by in the blink of an eye. I wanted to savor every last moment I had.

"Can we walk back to the hotel, Max?"

"Sure." He slid an arm around my waist.

As we walked I took in the lights and activity of Dublin nightlife. It was fascinating to discover new places and meet new people. Having a child would likely limit that. Maybe Max was right and I'd just let myself get caught up in a silly idea.

When we reached the hotel I ran a bath while Max settled at the computer.

Warm water cascaded down over my feet as I settled into the tub. The sound and sensation reminded me of the waterfall. I closed my eyes and recalled the rainbow. There were so many memories throughout our trip that were priceless to me. As the water rose my body began to relax. Yes there was a lot more ahead of us, but as long as we greeted it together, I knew we would be just fine.

Max poked his head into the bathroom. "I'm going to go to bed."

"Okay, I'll be out in a little while. Good night, Max. I love you."

"I love you too." He closed the door.

# CHAPTER 28

I lingered in the bathtub until the water grew cold, then I wrapped a robe around myself and stepped out of the bathroom. I noticed that Max had left the journal out on my pillow. He was already snoring, but he hadn't forgotten about his request.

I picked up the journal without any intention of telling the truth. But as I began to write, my emotions flowed. I wrote about my sudden desire for children and the beauty of the connections I'd been seeing around me between mothers and their babies. I wrote about the things that I imagined we could do together as a family. I also wrote about the parts that I was scared of experiencing—labor, the baby getting sick, diaper explosions, and just not being a good enough mother. At the end of all that I'd written, I drew a line and wrote beneath it:

*But more than anything, Max, I want you to be happy. Our lives can be full and joyful, regardless of whether or not we have a child. If it's not what you want, I hope that you will be honest with me.*

I slid the journal under his pillow, then settled into mine. With all my emotions out on that piece of paper I was able to fall asleep rather quickly.

When I woke up the next morning Max was already out of bed and in the shower. I looked at his pillow and could see the journal peeking out from under it. Had he read it? Had he forgotten about it?

My nerves felt a bit rattled as I dressed.

When Max emerged from the bathroom he was already dressed.

"Morning, most beautiful woman in Ireland."

"Ha."

"Just say thank you." He kissed my forehead.

"Thank you. Should we get some breakfast?"

"Let's skip it. We can pick up something when we get there."

"Get where?"

"I signed up for a tour of a castle. How can we be here and not see a castle?"

"Well, we did see a bit of a castle—must I remind you..." I stifled a giggle. "Please don't let me relive the nightmare of the Blarney Castle."

"Exactly. That doesn't count because we never made it past the main event there. My queen needs to get a glimpse of the way it once was."

"Queen, now?" I laughed. "I think I could get used to

this."

"You should." He slapped my rear end and pointed to the door. "Now move it, lass."

"Hm. I think you need to work on your accent."

"I think I'm going to work on my swatting if you don't get going." He arched a brow.

"You're not scary, Max."

"Not even a little bit?" He pouted.

"Not even at all." I laughed.

He grabbed my hand and tugged me toward the door. "The day awaits, let's greet it."

I was fairly certain that he hadn't read the journal. Otherwise, I assumed, we would have been having a much different conversation.

As Max claimed, he'd signed us up for a tour. The bus itself was fairly rickety, but the driver applied the gas in such a delicate way that I didn't notice a single bump. Max pointed out his favorite spots along the way and I did as well. When the bus came to a stop all of the other tourists on board filed off.

Max held me back for a moment. "I want you to really enjoy this, okay? No worries about Thailand or anything else. Can you do that?"

"Yes, I think I can. As long as I'm with you."

"Good." He squeezed my hand.

Once off the bus we had the option of roaming or joining the guided tour. Max and I didn't even have to discuss what we preferred. We began to roam. Although the castle was mostly intact there were a few places that had crumbled. Max and I competed to take the best picture. Then we started snapping silly selfies in different areas of the castle.

By the time we boarded the bus I was wiped out and the bagel we'd picked up along the way was not holding back the gnawing in my stomach.

As soon as we were off the bus we headed for a pub. Max ordered a Guinness and I decided to join him. As we toasted with our frothy drinks, he looked into my eyes.

"I wish I could give you a castle."

"I don't want a castle." I grinned.

"I still wish I could give you one."

"I'd rather have this—right now. You and me. That's all I need."

"Is it?" He sipped his drink then set it down.

"Sure it is, Max."

"It doesn't have to be. You know that, right?"

"What do you mean?" I held my breath, as I hoped that he'd read the journal and decided that he wanted kids after all.

"I mean, I don't want you to think that you have to appease me in some way. I'm here, I'm not going anywhere. If there are things that you want, that you think I won't agree with, I still want to hear about them."

"You mean kids?" I gripped the edge of the bar.

"Yes—that and anything else that you're concerned about."

"Max, I would never do anything to risk our relationship."

"But that's the point—there is no risk. I want you to understand that. Nothing will ever come between us. Don't you believe that?"

"I'm trying." I took a long swallow of my drink.

He glanced at his watch. "We have to get going if we're going to be ready for the book signing, but I want to talk about this more, alright?"

"Sure." I nodded. "After the tour and after we travel, right?"

"Sammy, don't." He brought my hand to his lips and kissed it. "Everything is going to be just fine."

# CHAPTER 29

I wanted to believe Max, but I wasn't sure if I should. Why would he just toy with me and not tell me if he'd read the journal? Why wouldn't he just come right out and say whether or not he wanted to have kids? I tried to put it out of my mind and focus on the book signing.

After a little time I was able to finally get my head back into the game. However, that little bit of beer left me more on edge. All of the old insecurities flooded back over me. They bubbled up, and I couldn't hold them back.

"Is it the weight, Max?" I blurted the question out as I met his eyes.

"What?" He picked up his laptop bag and slung it over his shoulder. "We have to go."

"I mean, is that what you're worried about? That I'll put too much weight back on? I can work out during the pregnancy."

"Sammy. You know me better than that." He leaned over to kiss me on the cheek. "And no, of course not, darling. But this isn't the time to talk about it. Let's get through this last event here, okay?"

My heart sank. Yes, he'd read the journal. And no, he still didn't want kids.

When we arrived at the final book signing, I tried to psych myself up for it. There was no need for me to feel insecure. All of these people were there because they appreciated my work and supported me. It should have been a confidence booster. But a crowd was a crowd in that moment, and I clung to Max's hand. I'm sure he sensed my nervousness but he didn't say a word. He just squeezed my hand and smiled at me.

Fiona rushed over. "Are you ready for this, Sammy? We're more packed than we were last night."

"I'm ready." I nodded, though I didn't feel ready at all.

When I walked up on the stage, I noticed that there was a large man sitting in the front row. He held the hand of a petite woman beside him. He drew my attention because it was unusual for a man like him to be one of my readers. I assumed he was there for his girlfriend. I invited questions, and the man's hand was the first one to shoot up.

"Yes, sir?"

He stared at me with just the corners of his lips turned upward. I couldn't tell if he was smiling or smirking.

"While we're waiting for your new book, my girlfriend and I have been following your blog. I think it's pretty amazing how you've developed your relationship with your husband. What do you think is the key to a good relationship?"

The question surprised me. Of all the things I thought he might ask, that was not one of them.

"I think honesty and communication are the most important things to me. If you can't trust the one you love, if you can't be one hundred percent yourself with them, then I don't see how you can be successful in your relationship."

"Thank you." He nodded and sat back down. His girlfriend smiled at him and the two whispered for a moment before the session continued.

After the reading, I sat at the table for quite a long time to sign the books of everyone who'd attended. It wasn't a tedious activity for me. I looked into the eyes of each reader and offered a smile of gratitude. How could this many people be interested in something that I'd written? It made my confidence soar.

After the crowd cleared out, Fiona caught up to me. "I know this is last-minute, but if you and Max don't have anything else planned for tonight, I'd love for you to come to my house for dinner. I'll make you some real Irish stew, not the kind you get at the restaurants."

"Thanks, Fiona, that would be wonderful. Let me just grab Max."

Max slid the last chair back into place then smiled at me. "What? More dancing?"

"No, no more dancing." I rubbed my thigh. "I don't think I can take any more. Fiona invited us to dinner. Want to go?"

"Sure. I'd love to."

I almost asked him about the journal. It was on my mind and made it to the tip of my tongue, but I thought it would be best to wait until after we'd visited with Fiona.

We followed Fiona to her home. It was larger than Shauna's but had the same general layout. As soon as we stepped inside, her two young girls rushed to the door.

Fiona smiled and held up a hand to stop them. "These are my daughters. I'm so glad that they have the chance to meet you. They're also big fans of your work."

I looked at the two teenagers and tried not to let my smile crack. Could two girls so young be interested in anything I had to say? "It's nice to meet you both."

"You too. We love your book and your blog." The taller girl grinned. "So do most of the girls in our class."

"Really? You connect with the book?"

"Oh, the book? No, not really." The shorter girl shrugged. "No offense, but I'm not that into fiction. We love your blog the most."

"Oh, I see—I'm glad that you do." I smiled.

"It's pretty well put together, right?" Max elbowed me.

"Sure, it's great," she said, "but it's the content that really counts. Every time I log in I feel like I'm living a little part of your life with you."

"I'm glad that it's had that much of an impact on you. That means a lot to me."

"Girls, come help me get dinner ready. Sammy and Max, make yourselves at home."

Max gestured to an overstuffed couch.

I sat down and he sat down beside me. In the quiet that surrounded us, I thought again about bringing up the topic of the journal.

"Max, I think we need to talk about something."

"Maybe, but this might not be the time." He tipped his head toward the two heads that poked out of the kitchen to spy on us in the living room.

I smiled. "You're right." I laced my fingers through his and looked around at the living room. It had a very lived-in feel—from the marks on the walls to the wear in the carpet. I was certainly never one to be spic and span, but now I understood even more what those marks meant. It meant that life was too busy to keep up with tidiness. It meant that memories were being made instead of beds.

That now all-too-familiar pang returned to my heart. Was this really something I wanted to miss out on?

"Dinner is served!"

We followed the delicious scent into the dining room. As Shauna promised, the Irish stew tasted far better than what we'd been served in the restaurants. In fact, there were elements of it that I didn't quite recognize but was certain needed to be there, as the flavor that filled my mouth was amazing.

"Fiona, have you ever considered moving to America?" Max looked across the table at her. "Because I don't think I can live without this in my life."

"Sorry, Max, if you want my cooking you have to come see me." She grinned.

"Well, we might do some traveling." I took another bite of the stew.

"We might." He looked over at me. "Or we might do other things."

I eyed him for a moment, unsure of what his comment meant. Luckily the girls began to argue about who'd made the better biscuits and whether Max would like them.

In fact, most of the dinner conversation was the two teenagers biting back and forth at one another. I enjoyed their creative insults and careful wording to avoid their mother's wrath.

After we finished dinner, the girls herded us toward the door. "We have something to show you—that we think you'll like."

Max and I followed after them. After a short walk we came upon a very large pond. It was filled with moss and fish that we could hear splashing in the distance.

"It's not anything spectacular, but it's our favorite place in Ireland," the eldest of the girls said.

"It's wonderful. Thank you for showing us." I slipped my hand into Max's.

"Girls! Come in now!"

I glanced back toward the house, where Fiona called from the front door.

"Coming!" The two girls ran back toward the house.

# CHAPTER 30

Max held my hand tight in his and looked into my eyes. "Can we stay here for a few minutes?"

"Sure." I leaned close to him. "I love these moments with you."

"So do I."

"They're good girls, aren't they? Sometimes I forget that teenagers can be just as sweet as young children."

"Yes, they can. Or they can be as wild as we were."

"I wasn't wild!"

"Maybe not, but you wanted to be." He grinned.

"I'm just saying, maybe the teenage years aren't as bad as people claim."

"Maybe not." He kissed my cheek.

"You don't want to talk about it, do you?"

"About what? Teenagers?" He shook his head. "Not really."

"Max, I don't want anything to create a barrier between us."

"Nothing ever could." He pulled me close for a kiss.

When I pulled away he stared into my eyes. "I read

the journal. I didn't want to write you back there. I wanted to speak to you about this face-to-face."

"You don't have to really. I understand."

"No—clearly, you don't." He took both of my hands in his. "Sammy, I love everything about you. I want our lives to be rich and our experiences to be filled with love. Children would only add to that."

"Really? I thought you didn't want—"

"I want us to be together. I adore every little thing about you. How could I not want more of you in the world? A little Sammy, taking the world by storm, just like her mother does? I would never turn that down."

"Or a little Max, with a heart of gold, just like his daddy?" I smiled.

"Oh boy, I don't know if I can handle a little me. I know what I did to my mother." Max grimaced, then laughed. "It's our adventure, Sammy. We get to decide where it takes us. The way you described how you're feeling made me realize that I feel that way too. I guess I just assumed our lives were settled—that you wouldn't want to change that with children."

"Children?" I grinned. "How many?"

"I think we'll figure that out together. When you're ready, I'm ready. Okay?" He drew my hand to his lips and kissed it.

"But don't you think it will change our lives too much? What about your freedom?"

"I don't need anything but you."

"My body would change and—"

"Sammy." He cupped my cheeks and gazed into my eyes. "No matter how your body changes, even when we're buried in soiled diapers, even when there is absolutely no way that we think we're going to make it, you are going to be the most beautiful woman I have ever laid eyes on. I never want you to worry about that. Understand?"

I nodded and turned my lips into his palm. When I kissed it, I was reminded of just how safe I always felt with him. "I love you."

"I love you too, Sammy. You will be an amazing mother." He winced. "Me, on the other hand, I might need just a little help in the daddy department."

"I think you'd be a natural."

"I guess we'll find out—when we're ready. We'll talk about all of it after the book tour, alright?"

"Yes." I stared into his eyes and suddenly believed in leprechauns and magic again.

Max was my pot of gold at the end of the rainbow— my treasure in life. He'd always been that for me, and I knew from listening to his sweet words that I was his treasure also.

LILLIANNA BLAKE

# A NOTE FROM THE AUTHOR

Fictional character, Samantha Bradford and the Single Wide Female books are written for every woman out there who has struggled with their weight, self-esteem and any number of issues that we all face as we work to become the best versions of ourselves that we can be.

These books are meant to be light-hearted and fun, with the hope that they will also inspire you to make your own "bucket list" of sorts—and to REALLY live your life to the fullest, loving yourself completely as you do so.

Lillianna loves to hear from her readers and can be contacted via her website where you can also download a complimentary book.

LilliannaBlake.com

# ALL TITLES BY LILLIANNA BLAKE

http://Amazon.com/author/lilliannablake
*Check the author page for current list of titles

## Single Wide Female: The Bucket List

#1 Learn Pole Dancing

#2 Start a Blog

#3 Learn to Cook

#4 Create a Masterpiece

#5 Run a Marathon

#6 Go Skinny Dipping

#7 Start Online Dating

#8 Learn Yoga

#9 Be a Mentor

#10 Crash a Wedding

#11 Be a Movie Extra

#12 Join a Writing Group

#13 Enjoy a Spa Day

#14 Donate Blood

#15 Learn Poker

#16 Get a Tattoo

#17 Host a Dinner Party

#18 Publish a Book

#19 Walk Across Hot Coals

#20 Learn to Swim

#21 Learn to Meditate

#22 Quit My Job

#23 Learn to Salsa

#24 Fall in Love

Visit the author website at LilliannaBlake.com to get on the notification list for new releases and to receive a complimentary book to learn what inspired Sammy to begin her bucket list.

www.ingramcontent.com/pod-product-compliance
Lightning Source LLC
Chambersburg PA
CBHW060945180626
46817CB00004B/1714